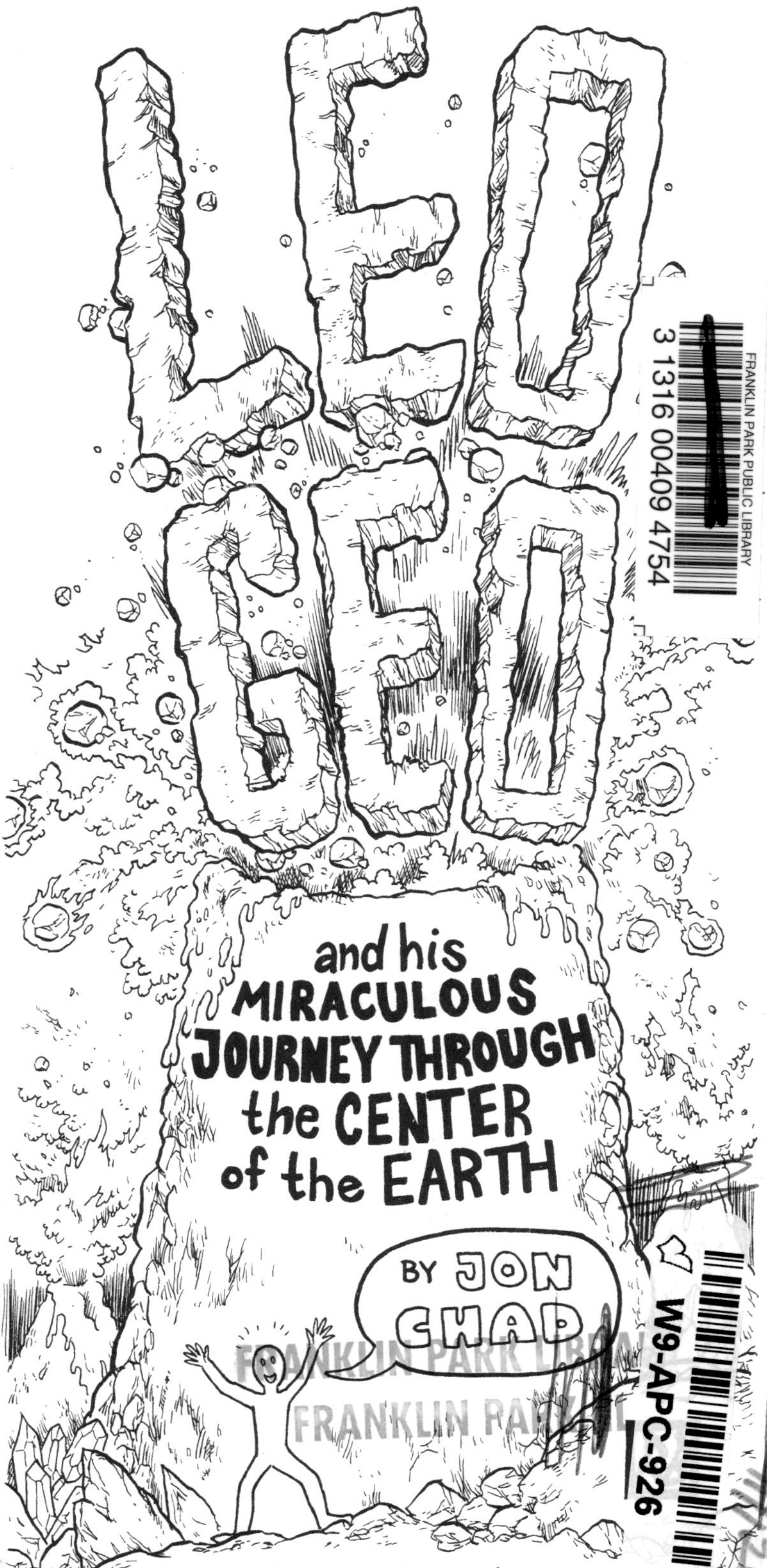
LEO GEO
and his
MIRACULOUS
JOURNEY THROUGH
the CENTER
of the EARTH
BY JON CHAD

Roaring Brook Press • New York

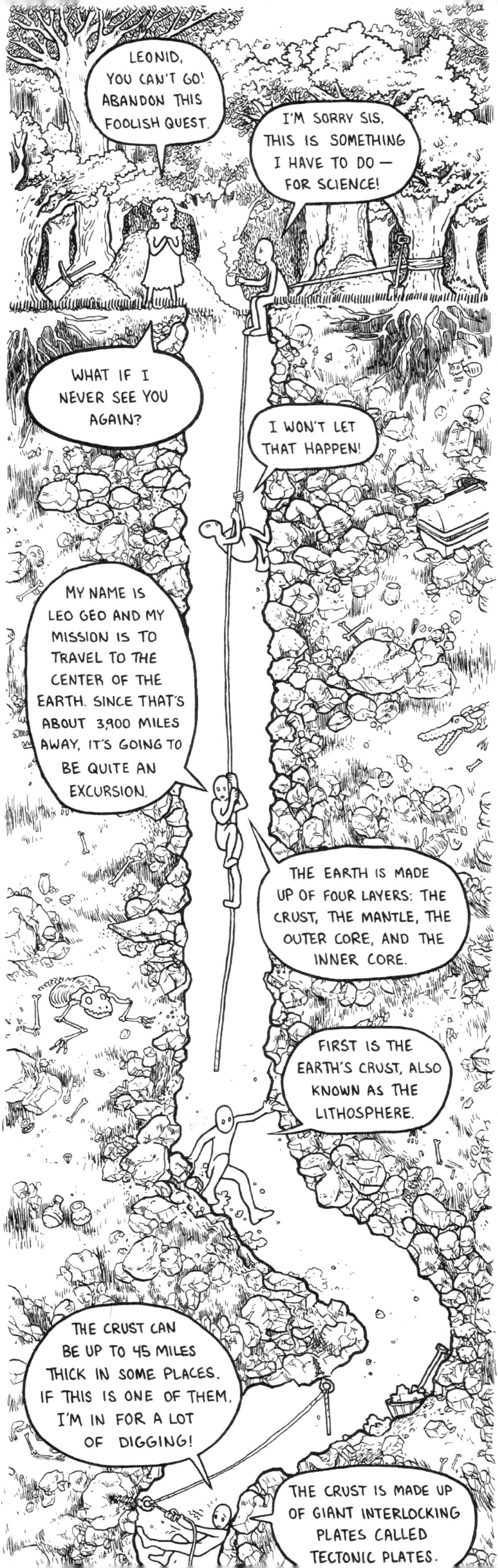
LEONID, YOU CAN'T GO! ABANDON THIS FOOLISH QUEST.
I'M SORRY SIS, THIS IS SOMETHING I HAVE TO DO — FOR SCIENCE!
WHAT IF I NEVER SEE YOU AGAIN?
I WON'T LET THAT HAPPEN!
MY NAME IS LEO GEO AND MY MISSION IS TO TRAVEL TO THE CENTER OF THE EARTH. SINCE THAT'S ABOUT 3,900 MILES AWAY, IT'S GOING TO BE QUITE AN EXCURSION.
THE EARTH IS MADE UP OF FOUR LAYERS: THE CRUST, THE MANTLE, THE OUTER CORE, AND THE INNER CORE.
FIRST IS THE EARTH'S CRUST, ALSO KNOWN AS THE LITHOSPHERE.
THE CRUST CAN BE UP TO 45 MILES THICK IN SOME PLACES. IF THIS IS ONE OF THEM, I'M IN FOR A LOT OF DIGGING!
THE CRUST IS MADE UP OF GIANT INTERLOCKING PLATES CALLED TECTONIC PLATES.

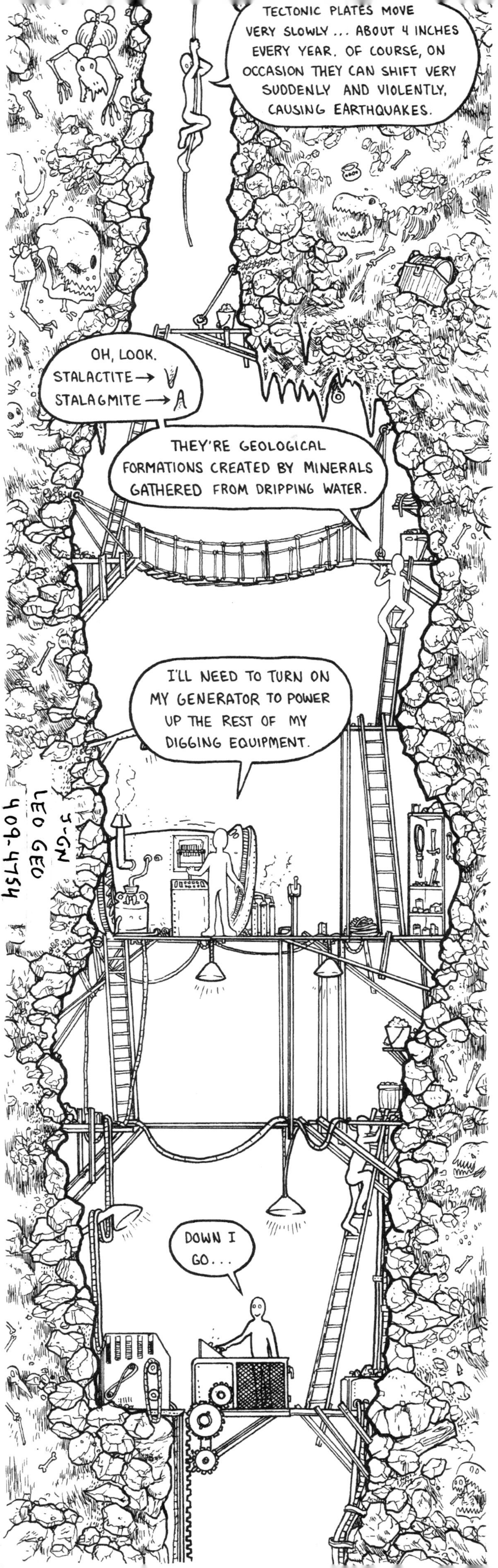
TECTONIC PLATES MOVE VERY SLOWLY... ABOUT 4 INCHES EVERY YEAR. OF COURSE, ON OCCASION THEY CAN SHIFT VERY SUDDENLY AND VIOLENTLY, CAUSING EARTHQUAKES.
OH, LOOK.
STALACTITE →
STALAGMITE →
THEY'RE GEOLOGICAL FORMATIONS CREATED BY MINERALS GATHERED FROM DRIPPING WATER.
I'LL NEED TO TURN ON MY GENERATOR TO POWER UP THE REST OF MY DIGGING EQUIPMENT.
DOWN I GO...

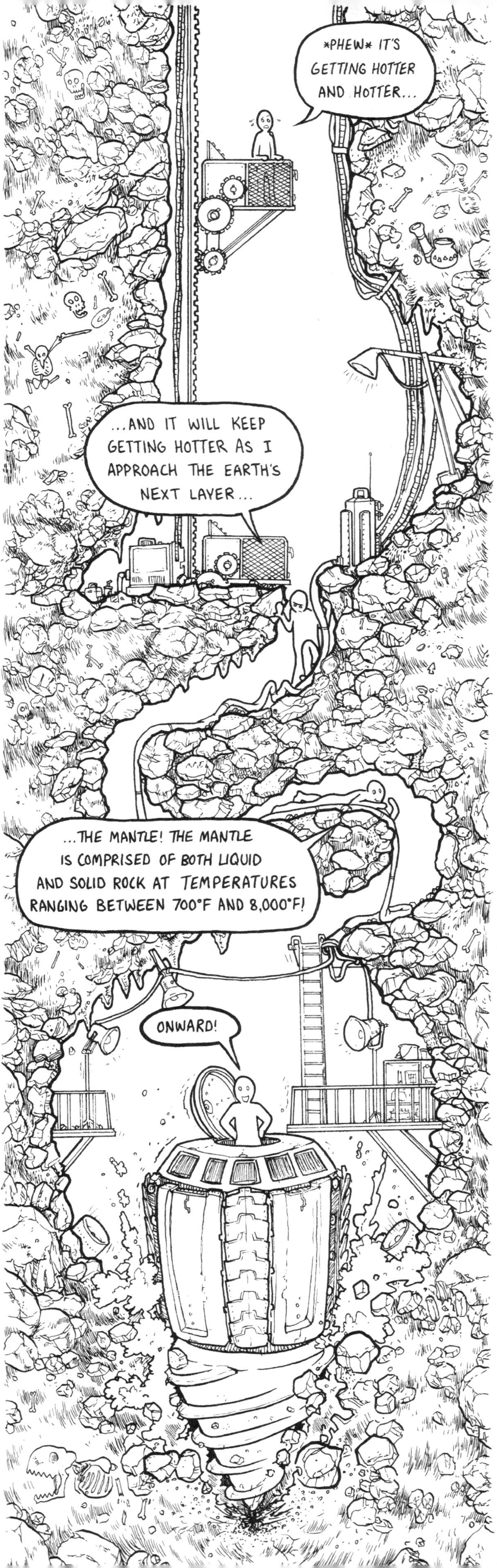
PHEW IT'S GETTING HOTTER AND HOTTER...
...AND IT WILL KEEP GETTING HOTTER AS I APPROACH THE EARTH'S NEXT LAYER...
...THE MANTLE! THE MANTLE IS COMPRISED OF BOTH LIQUID AND SOLID ROCK AT TEMPERATURES RANGING BETWEEN 700°F AND 8,000°F!
ONWARD!

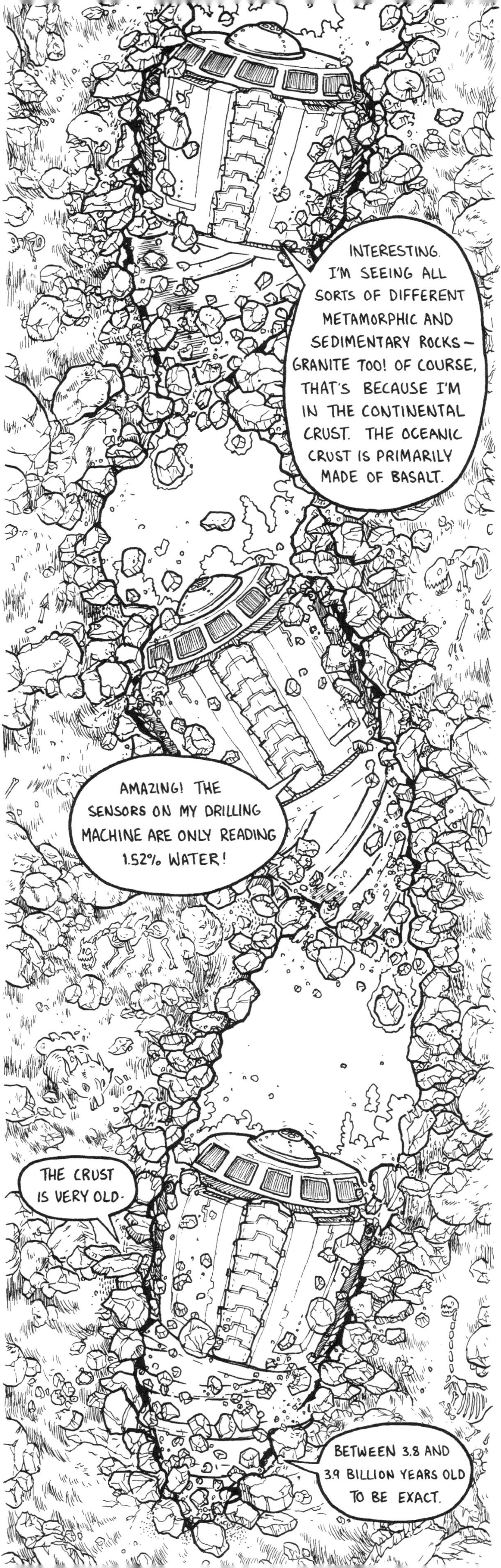
INTERESTING. I'M SEEING ALL SORTS OF DIFFERENT METAMORPHIC AND SEDIMENTARY ROCKS— GRANITE TOO! OF COURSE, THAT'S BECAUSE I'M IN THE CONTINENTAL CRUST. THE OCEANIC CRUST IS PRIMARILY MADE OF BASALT.
AMAZING! THE SENSORS ON MY DRILLING MACHINE ARE ONLY READING 1.52% WATER!
THE CRUST IS VERY OLD.
BETWEEN 3.8 AND 3.9 BILLION YEARS OLD TO BE EXACT.

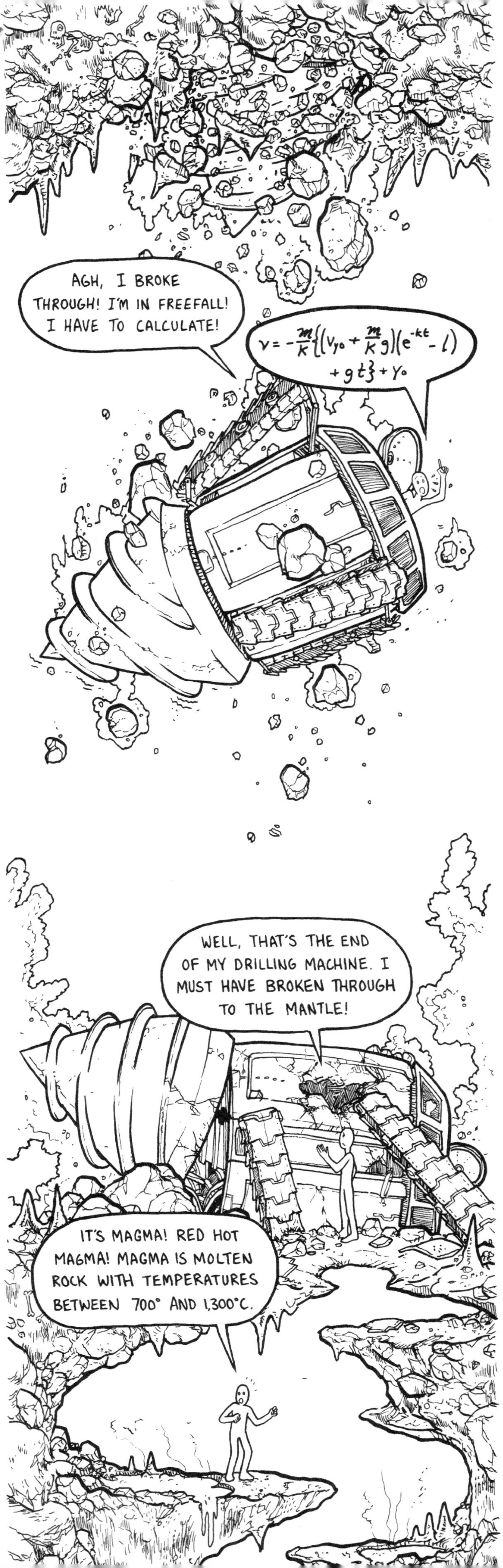
AGH, I BROKE THROUGH! I'M IN FREEFALL! I HAVE TO CALCULATE!
$y = -\frac{m}{k}\{(v_{y0} + \frac{m}{k}g)(e^{-kt} - 1) + gt\} + y_0$
WELL, THAT'S THE END OF MY DRILLING MACHINE. I MUST HAVE BROKEN THROUGH TO THE MANTLE!
IT'S MAGMA! RED HOT MAGMA! MAGMA IS MOLTEN ROCK WITH TEMPERATURES BETWEEN 700° AND 1,300°C.

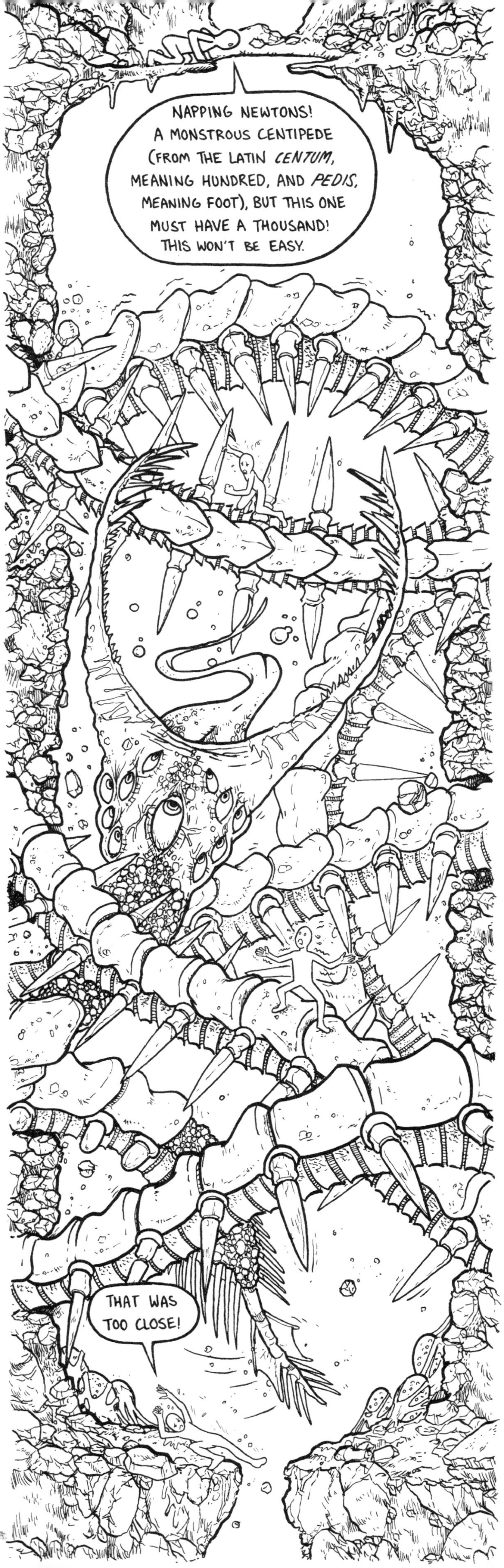
NAPPING NEWTONS! A MONSTROUS CENTIPEDE (FROM THE LATIN *CENTUM*, MEANING HUNDRED, AND *PEDIS*, MEANING FOOT), BUT THIS ONE MUST HAVE A THOUSAND! THIS WON'T BE EASY.
THAT WAS TOO CLOSE!

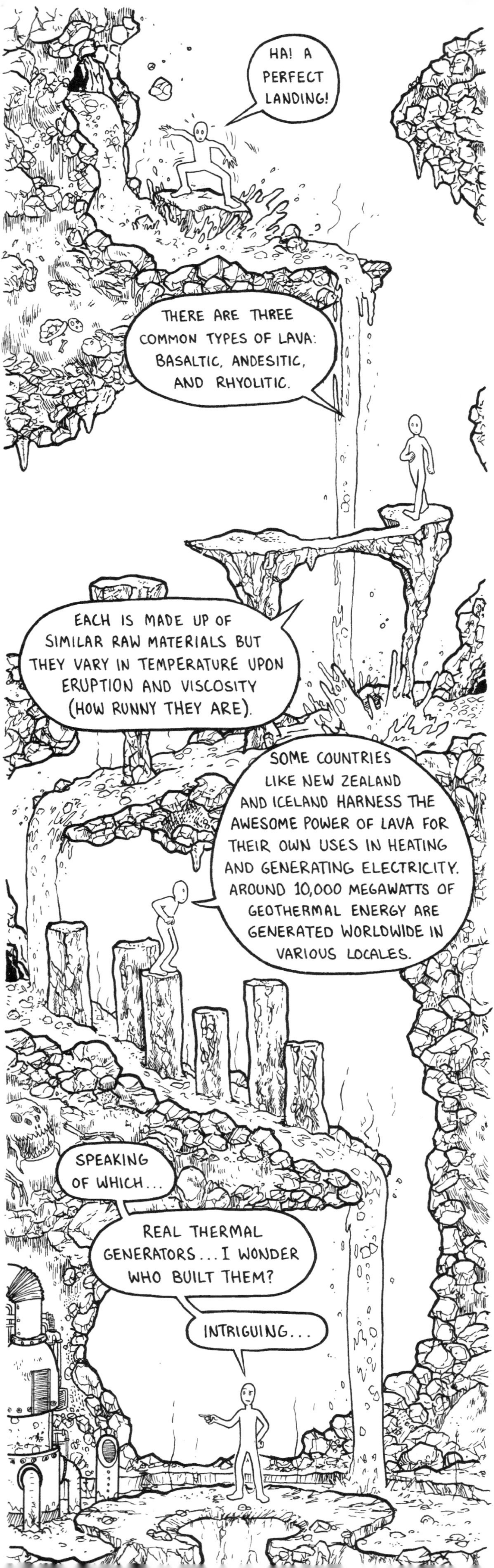
HA! A PERFECT LANDING!
THERE ARE THREE COMMON TYPES OF LAVA: BASALTIC, ANDESITIC, AND RHYOLITIC.
EACH IS MADE UP OF SIMILAR RAW MATERIALS BUT THEY VARY IN TEMPERATURE UPON ERUPTION AND VISCOSITY (HOW RUNNY THEY ARE).
SOME COUNTRIES LIKE NEW ZEALAND AND ICELAND HARNESS THE AWESOME POWER OF LAVA FOR THEIR OWN USES IN HEATING AND GENERATING ELECTRICITY. AROUND 10,000 MEGAWATTS OF GEOTHERMAL ENERGY ARE GENERATED WORLDWIDE IN VARIOUS LOCALES.
SPEAKING OF WHICH...
REAL THERMAL GENERATORS... I WONDER WHO BUILT THEM?
INTRIGUING...

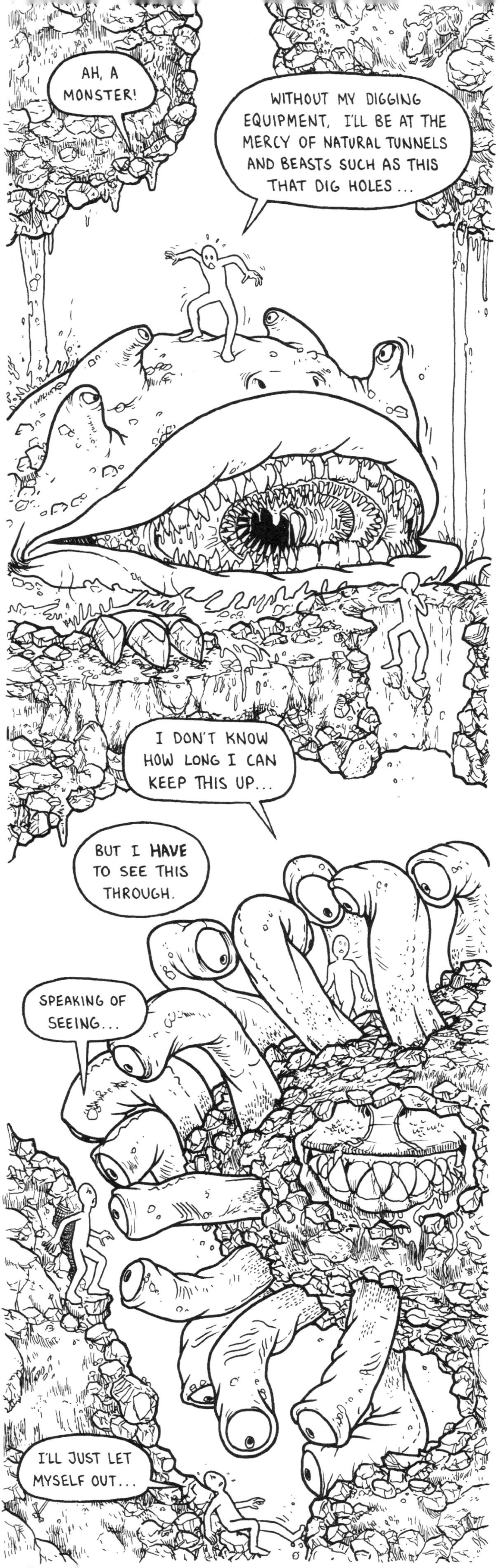
AH, A MONSTER!
WITHOUT MY DIGGING EQUIPMENT, I'LL BE AT THE MERCY OF NATURAL TUNNELS AND BEASTS SUCH AS THIS THAT DIG HOLES...
I DON'T KNOW HOW LONG I CAN KEEP THIS UP...
BUT I **HAVE** TO SEE THIS THROUGH.
SPEAKING OF SEEING...
I'LL JUST LET MYSELF OUT...

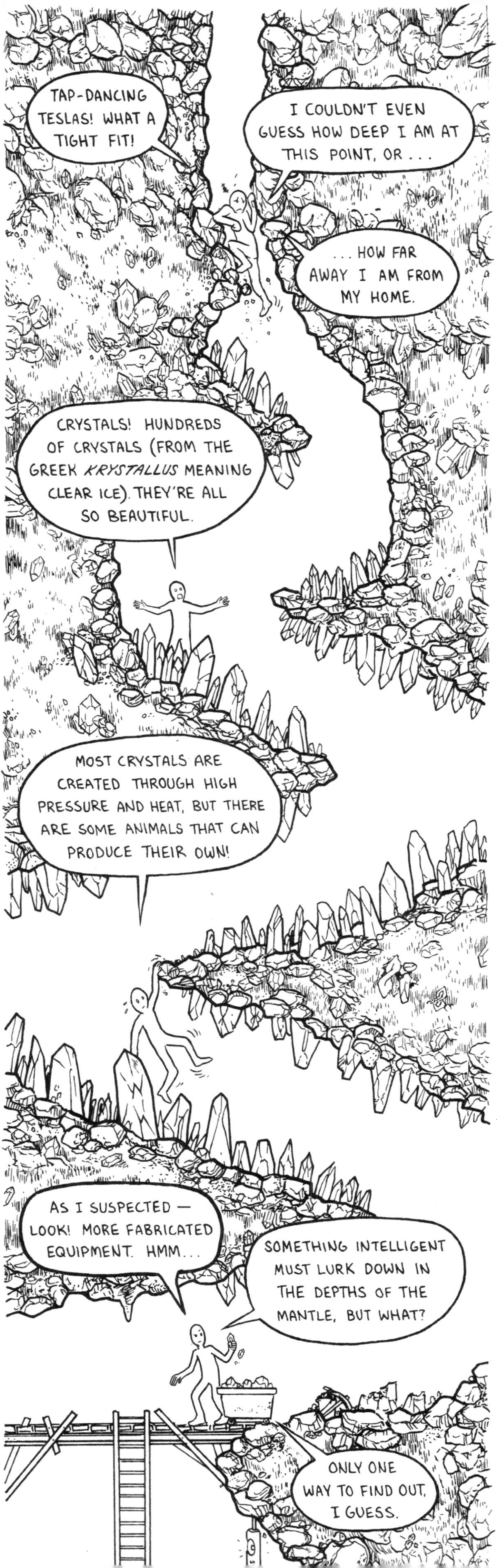
TAP-DANCING TESLAS! WHAT A TIGHT FIT!
I COULDN'T EVEN GUESS HOW DEEP I AM AT THIS POINT, OR . . .
. . . HOW FAR AWAY I AM FROM MY HOME.
CRYSTALS! HUNDREDS OF CRYSTALS (FROM THE GREEK *KRYSTALLUS* MEANING CLEAR ICE). THEY'RE ALL SO BEAUTIFUL.
MOST CRYSTALS ARE CREATED THROUGH HIGH PRESSURE AND HEAT, BUT THERE ARE SOME ANIMALS THAT CAN PRODUCE THEIR OWN!
AS I SUSPECTED — LOOK! MORE FABRICATED EQUIPMENT. HMM...
SOMETHING INTELLIGENT MUST LURK DOWN IN THE DEPTHS OF THE MANTLE, BUT WHAT?
ONLY ONE WAY TO FIND OUT, I GUESS.

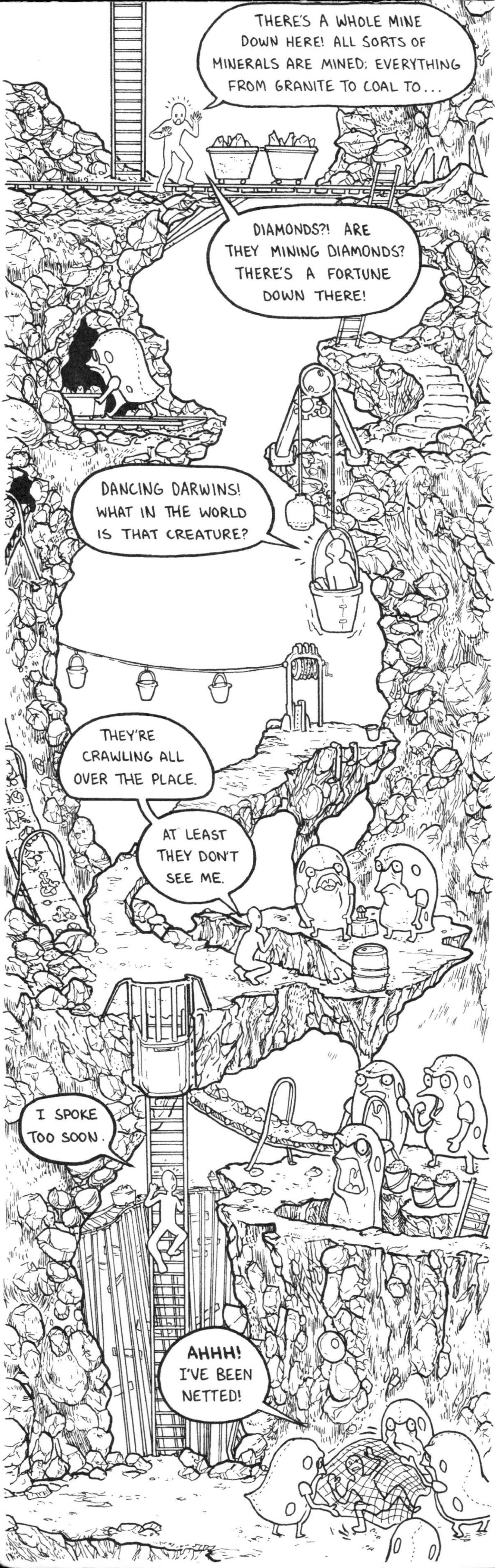
THERE'S A WHOLE MINE DOWN HERE! ALL SORTS OF MINERALS ARE MINED; EVERYTHING FROM GRANITE TO COAL TO...
DIAMONDS?! ARE THEY MINING DIAMONDS? THERE'S A FORTUNE DOWN THERE!
DANCING DARWINS! WHAT IN THE WORLD IS THAT CREATURE?
THEY'RE CRAWLING ALL OVER THE PLACE.
AT LEAST THEY DON'T SEE ME.
I SPOKE TOO SOON.
AHHH! I'VE BEEN NETTED!

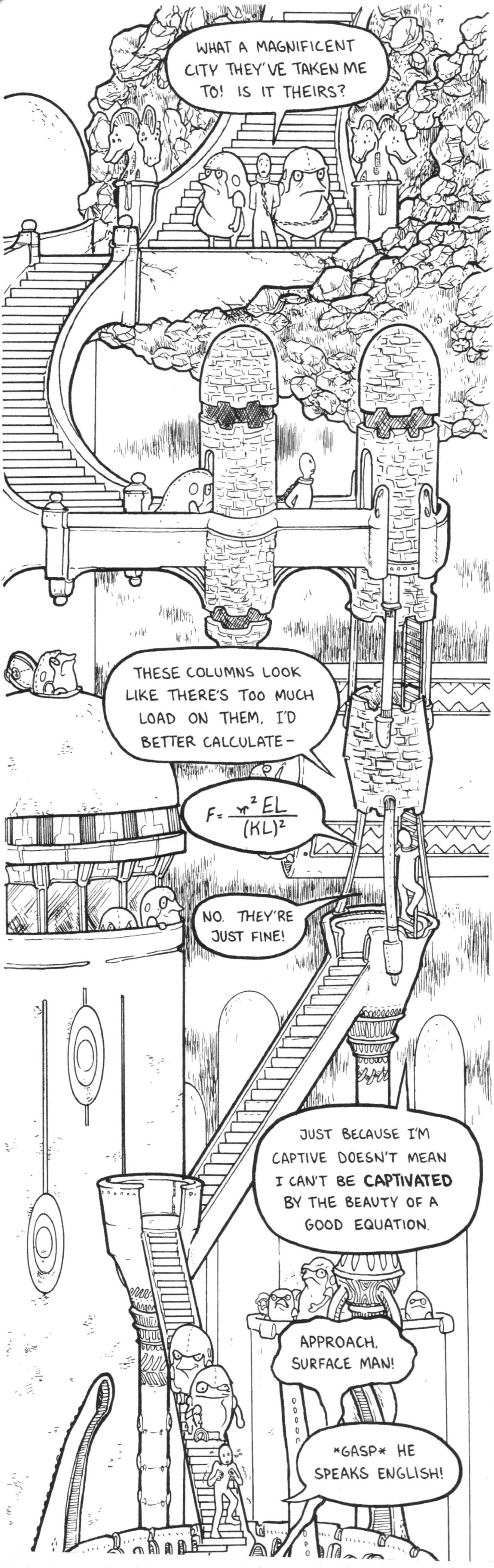
WHAT A MAGNIFICENT CITY THEY'VE TAKEN ME TO! IS IT THEIRS?
THESE COLUMNS LOOK LIKE THERE'S TOO MUCH LOAD ON THEM. I'D BETTER CALCULATE–
$F = \frac{\pi^2 EL}{(KL)^2}$
NO. THEY'RE JUST FINE!
JUST BECAUSE I'M CAPTIVE DOESN'T MEAN I CAN'T BE **CAPTIVATED** BY THE BEAUTY OF A GOOD EQUATION.
APPROACH, SURFACE MAN!
GASP HE SPEAKS ENGLISH!

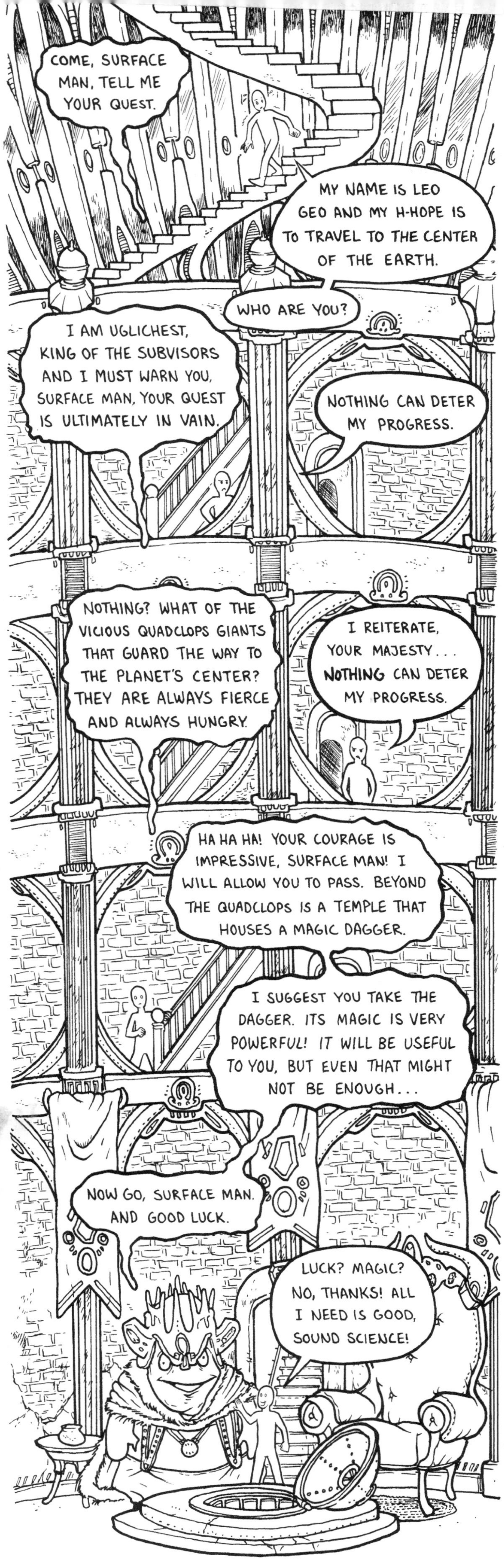
COME, SURFACE MAN, TELL ME YOUR QUEST.
MY NAME IS LEO GEO AND MY H-HOPE IS TO TRAVEL TO THE CENTER OF THE EARTH.
WHO ARE YOU?
I AM UGLICHEST, KING OF THE SUBVISORS AND I MUST WARN YOU, SURFACE MAN, YOUR QUEST IS ULTIMATELY IN VAIN.
NOTHING CAN DETER MY PROGRESS.
NOTHING? WHAT OF THE VICIOUS QUADCLOPS GIANTS THAT GUARD THE WAY TO THE PLANET'S CENTER? THEY ARE ALWAYS FIERCE AND ALWAYS HUNGRY.
I REITERATE, YOUR MAJESTY... **NOTHING** CAN DETER MY PROGRESS.
HA HA HA! YOUR COURAGE IS IMPRESSIVE, SURFACE MAN! I WILL ALLOW YOU TO PASS. BEYOND THE QUADCLOPS IS A TEMPLE THAT HOUSES A MAGIC DAGGER.
I SUGGEST YOU TAKE THE DAGGER. ITS MAGIC IS VERY POWERFUL! IT WILL BE USEFUL TO YOU, BUT EVEN THAT MIGHT NOT BE ENOUGH...
NOW GO, SURFACE MAN. AND GOOD LUCK.
LUCK? MAGIC? NO, THANKS! ALL I NEED IS GOOD, SOUND SCIENCE!

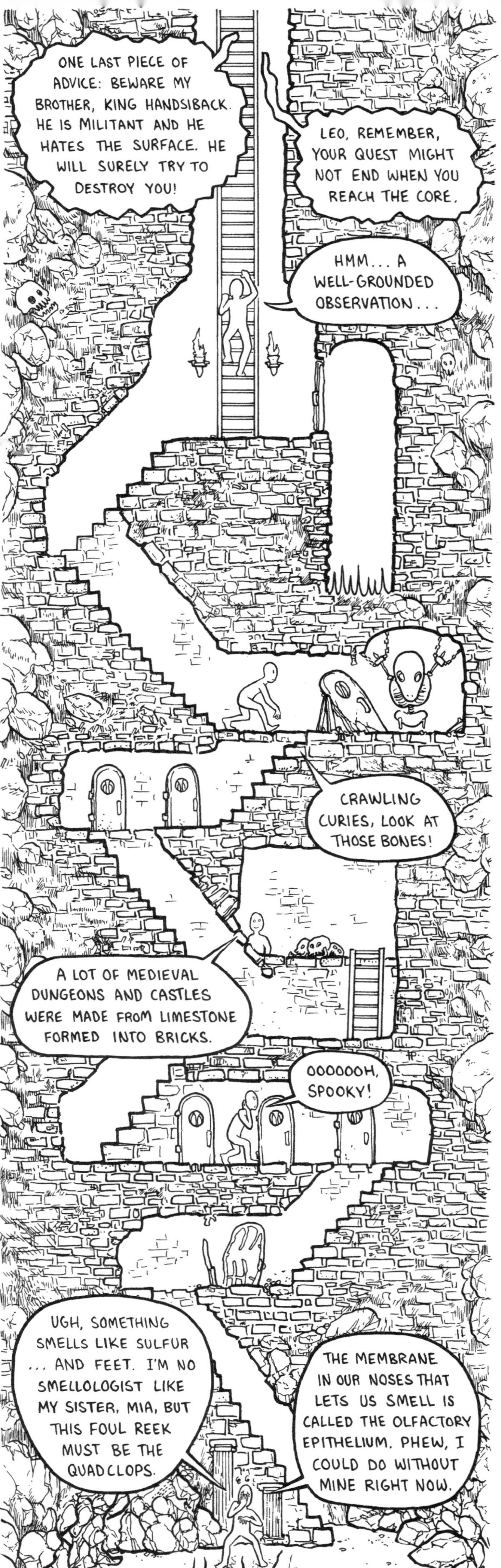
ONE LAST PIECE OF ADVICE: BEWARE MY BROTHER, KING HANDSIBACK. HE IS MILITANT AND HE HATES THE SURFACE. HE WILL SURELY TRY TO DESTROY YOU!
LEO, REMEMBER, YOUR QUEST MIGHT NOT END WHEN YOU REACH THE CORE.
HMM... A WELL-GROUNDED OBSERVATION...
CRAWLING CURIES, LOOK AT THOSE BONES!
A LOT OF MEDIEVAL DUNGEONS AND CASTLES WERE MADE FROM LIMESTONE FORMED INTO BRICKS.
OOOOOOH, SPOOKY!
UGH, SOMETHING SMELLS LIKE SULFUR ... AND FEET. I'M NO SMELLOLOGIST LIKE MY SISTER, MIA, BUT THIS FOUL REEK MUST BE THE QUADCLOPS.
THE MEMBRANE IN OUR NOSES THAT LETS US SMELL IS CALLED THE OLFACTORY EPITHELIUM. PHEW, I COULD DO WITHOUT MINE RIGHT NOW.

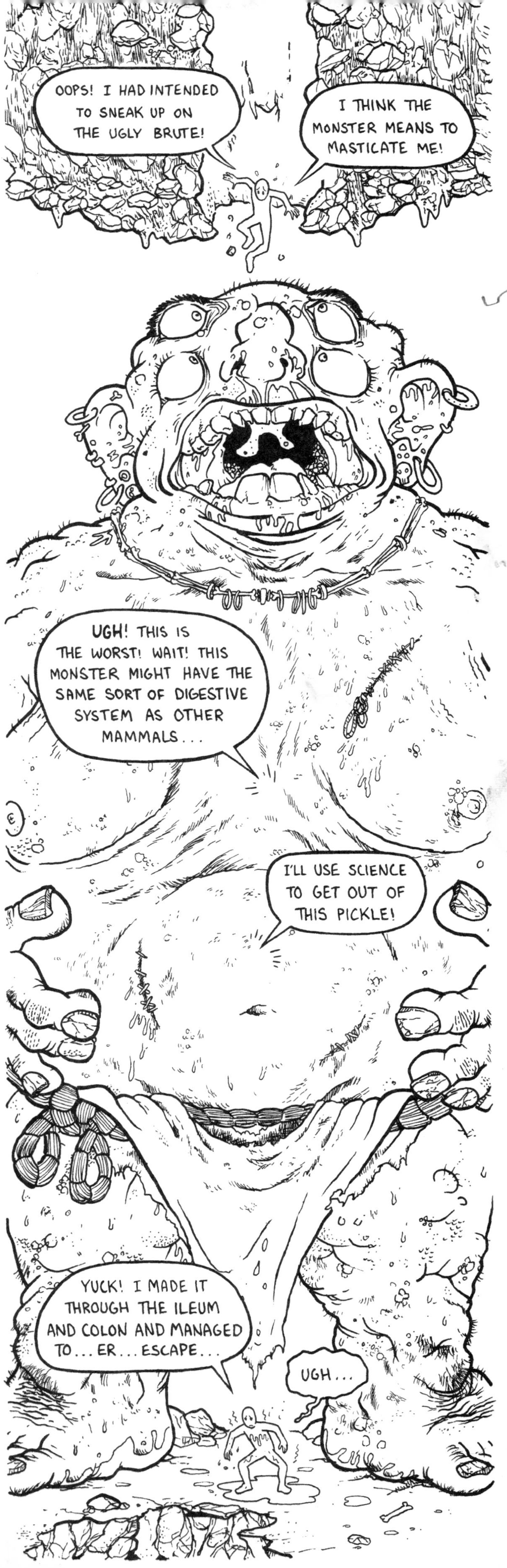
OOPS! I HAD INTENDED TO SNEAK UP ON THE UGLY BRUTE!
I THINK THE MONSTER MEANS TO MASTICATE ME!
UGH! THIS IS THE WORST! WAIT! THIS MONSTER MIGHT HAVE THE SAME SORT OF DIGESTIVE SYSTEM AS OTHER MAMMALS...
I'LL USE SCIENCE TO GET OUT OF THIS PICKLE!
YUCK! I MADE IT THROUGH THE ILEUM AND COLON AND MANAGED TO... ER... ESCAPE...
UGH...

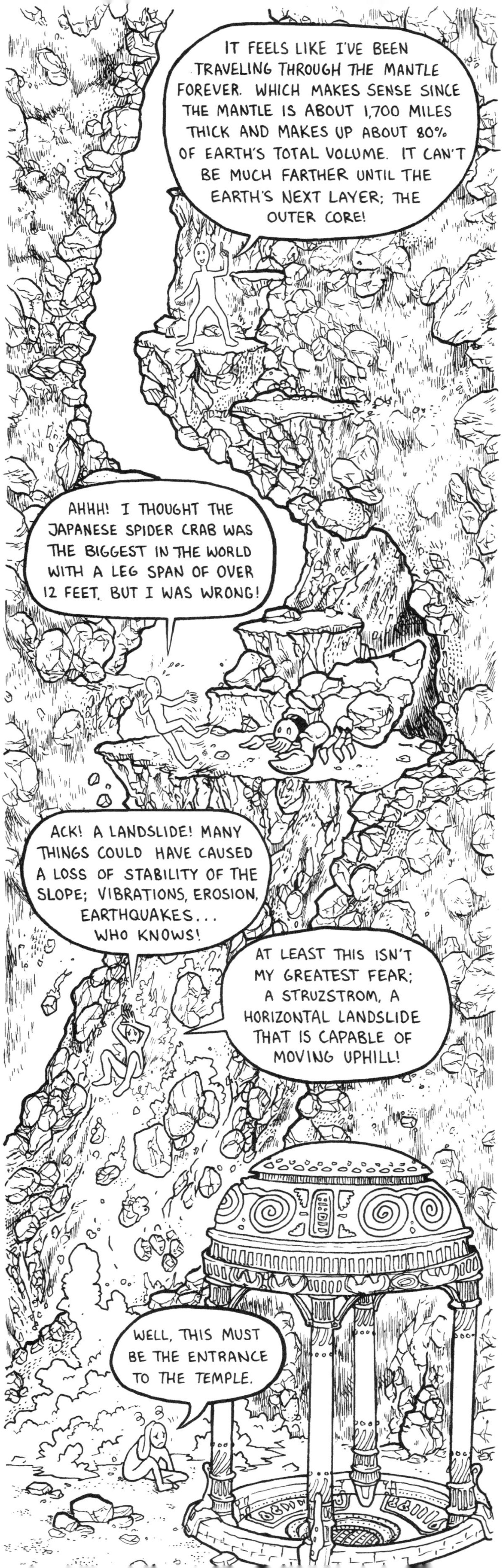
IT FEELS LIKE I'VE BEEN TRAVELING THROUGH THE MANTLE FOREVER. WHICH MAKES SENSE SINCE THE MANTLE IS ABOUT 1,700 MILES THICK AND MAKES UP ABOUT 80% OF EARTH'S TOTAL VOLUME. IT CAN'T BE MUCH FARTHER UNTIL THE EARTH'S NEXT LAYER; THE OUTER CORE!
AHHH! I THOUGHT THE JAPANESE SPIDER CRAB WAS THE BIGGEST IN THE WORLD WITH A LEG SPAN OF OVER 12 FEET, BUT I WAS WRONG!
ACK! A LANDSLIDE! MANY THINGS COULD HAVE CAUSED A LOSS OF STABILITY OF THE SLOPE; VIBRATIONS, EROSION, EARTHQUAKES... WHO KNOWS!
AT LEAST THIS ISN'T MY GREATEST FEAR; A STRUZSTROM, A HORIZONTAL LANDSLIDE THAT IS CAPABLE OF MOVING UPHILL!
WELL, THIS MUST BE THE ENTRANCE TO THE TEMPLE.

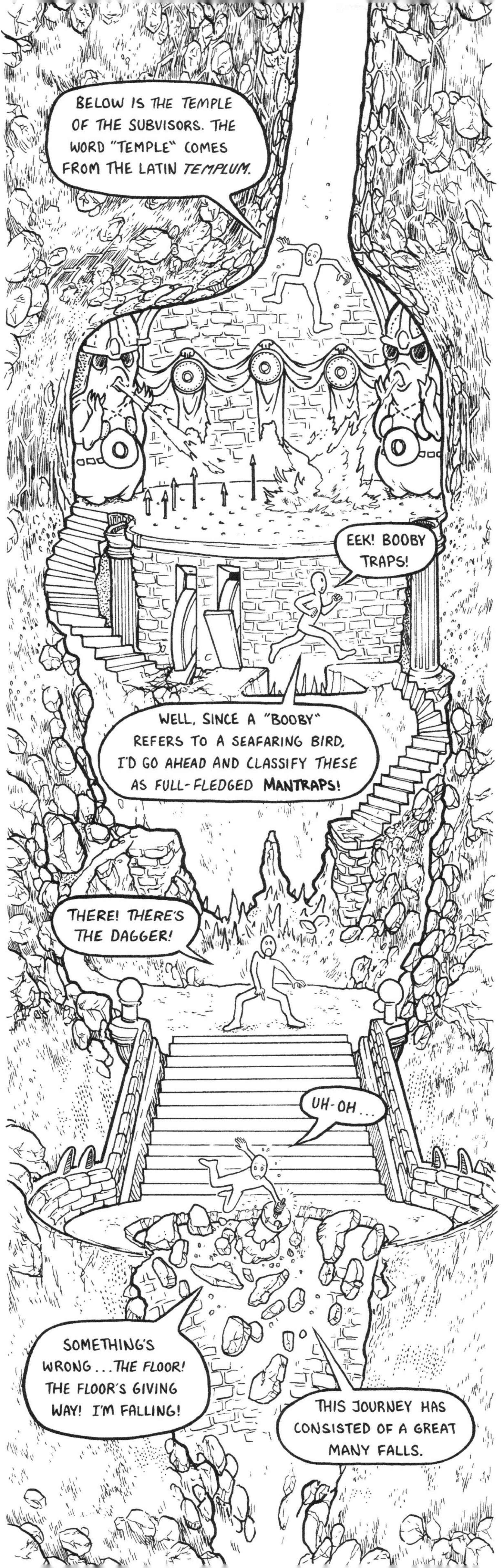
BELOW IS THE TEMPLE OF THE SUBVISORS. THE WORD "TEMPLE" COMES FROM THE LATIN *TEMPLUM*.
EEK! BOOBY TRAPS!
WELL, SINCE A "BOOBY" REFERS TO A SEAFARING BIRD, I'D GO AHEAD AND CLASSIFY THESE AS FULL-FLEDGED **MANTRAPS**!
THERE! THERE'S THE DAGGER!
UH-OH...
SOMETHING'S WRONG... THE FLOOR! THE FLOOR'S GIVING WAY! I'M FALLING!
THIS JOURNEY HAS CONSISTED OF A GREAT MANY FALLS.

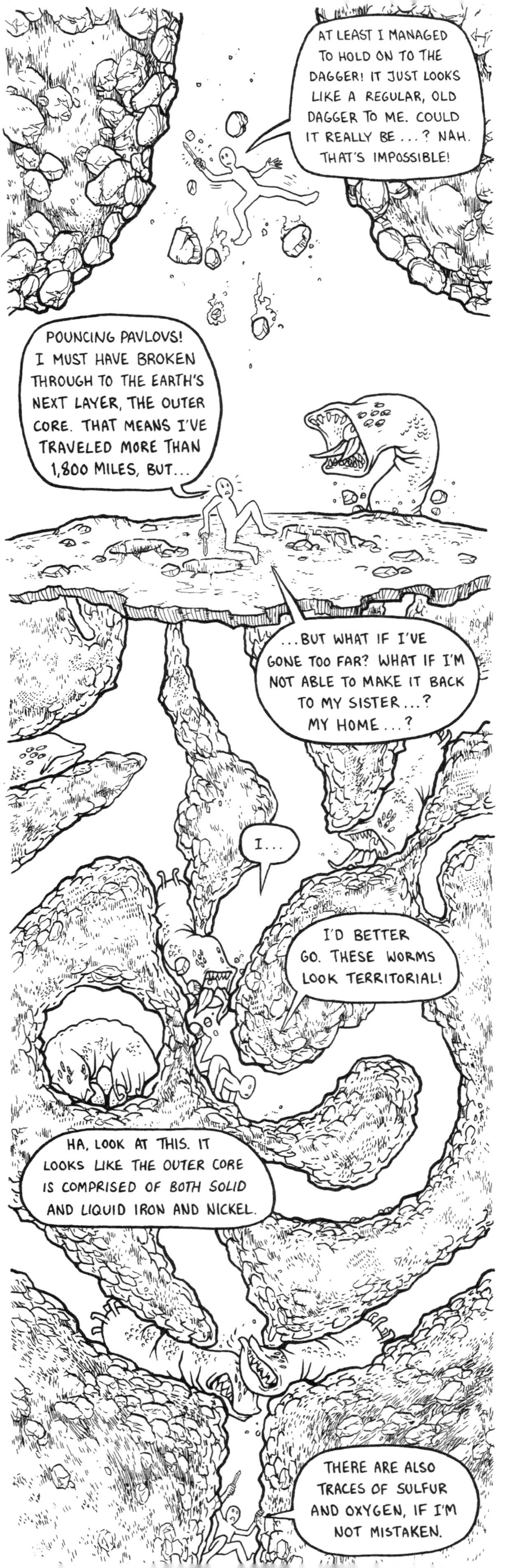
AT LEAST I MANAGED TO HOLD ON TO THE DAGGER! IT JUST LOOKS LIKE A REGULAR, OLD DAGGER TO ME. COULD IT REALLY BE . . . ? NAH. THAT'S IMPOSSIBLE!
POUNCING PAVLOVS! I MUST HAVE BROKEN THROUGH TO THE EARTH'S NEXT LAYER, THE OUTER CORE. THAT MEANS I'VE TRAVELED MORE THAN 1,800 MILES, BUT...
...BUT WHAT IF I'VE GONE TOO FAR? WHAT IF I'M NOT ABLE TO MAKE IT BACK TO MY SISTER...? MY HOME...?
I...
I'D BETTER GO. THESE WORMS LOOK TERRITORIAL!
HA, LOOK AT THIS. IT LOOKS LIKE THE OUTER CORE IS COMPRISED OF BOTH SOLID AND LIQUID IRON AND NICKEL.
THERE ARE ALSO TRACES OF SULFUR AND OXYGEN, IF I'M NOT MISTAKEN.

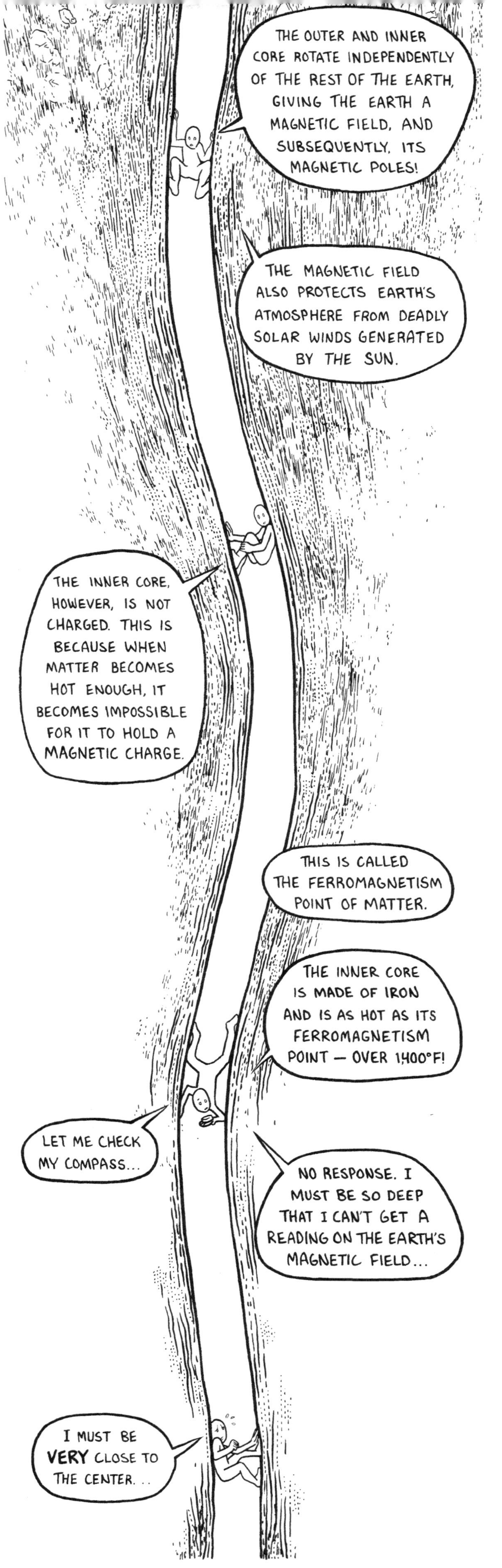
THE OUTER AND INNER CORE ROTATE INDEPENDENTLY OF THE REST OF THE EARTH, GIVING THE EARTH A MAGNETIC FIELD, AND SUBSEQUENTLY, ITS MAGNETIC POLES!
THE MAGNETIC FIELD ALSO PROTECTS EARTH'S ATMOSPHERE FROM DEADLY SOLAR WINDS GENERATED BY THE SUN.
THE INNER CORE, HOWEVER, IS NOT CHARGED. THIS IS BECAUSE WHEN MATTER BECOMES HOT ENOUGH, IT BECOMES IMPOSSIBLE FOR IT TO HOLD A MAGNETIC CHARGE.
THIS IS CALLED THE FERROMAGNETISM POINT OF MATTER.
THE INNER CORE IS MADE OF IRON AND IS AS HOT AS ITS FERROMAGNETISM POINT — OVER 1,400°F!
LET ME CHECK MY COMPASS...
NO RESPONSE. I MUST BE SO DEEP THAT I CAN'T GET A READING ON THE EARTH'S MAGNETIC FIELD...
I MUST BE **VERY** CLOSE TO THE CENTER...

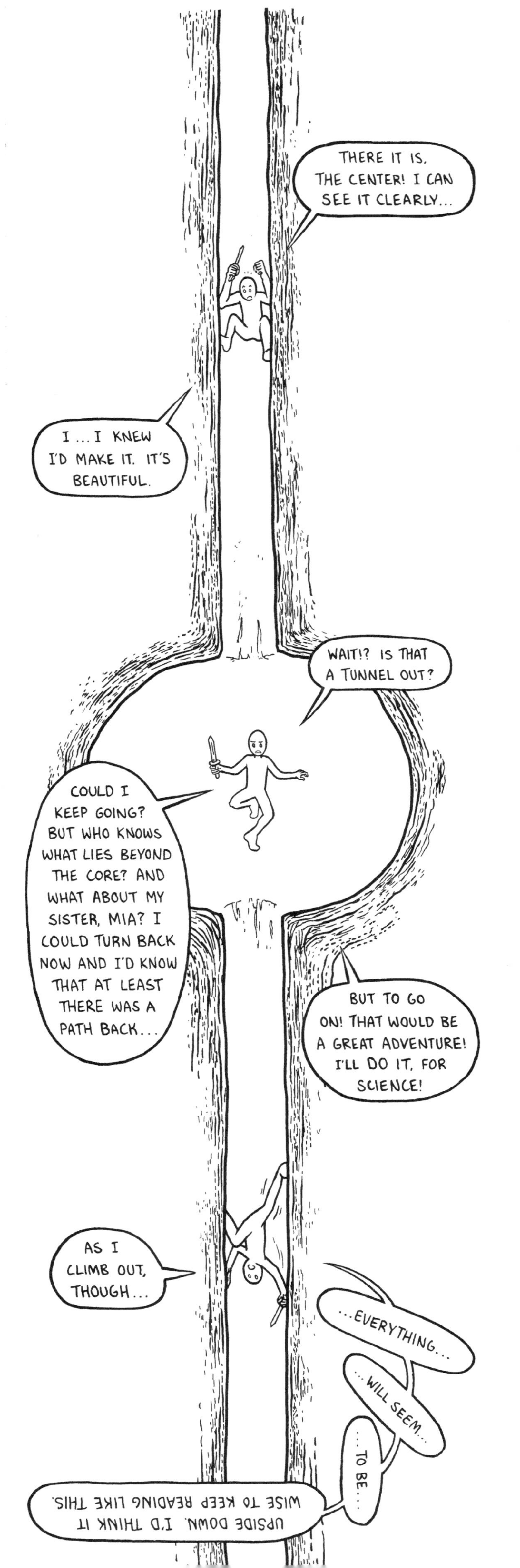
THERE IT IS. THE CENTER! I CAN SEE IT CLEARLY...
I ... I KNEW I'D MAKE IT. IT'S BEAUTIFUL.
WAIT!? IS THAT A TUNNEL OUT?
COULD I KEEP GOING? BUT WHO KNOWS WHAT LIES BEYOND THE CORE? AND WHAT ABOUT MY SISTER, MIA? I COULD TURN BACK NOW AND I'D KNOW THAT AT LEAST THERE WAS A PATH BACK...
BUT TO GO ON! THAT WOULD BE A GREAT ADVENTURE! I'LL DO IT, FOR SCIENCE!
AS I CLIMB OUT, THOUGH...
...EVERYTHING...
...WILL SEEM...
...TO BE...
UPSIDE DOWN. I'D THINK IT WISE TO KEEP READING LIKE THIS.

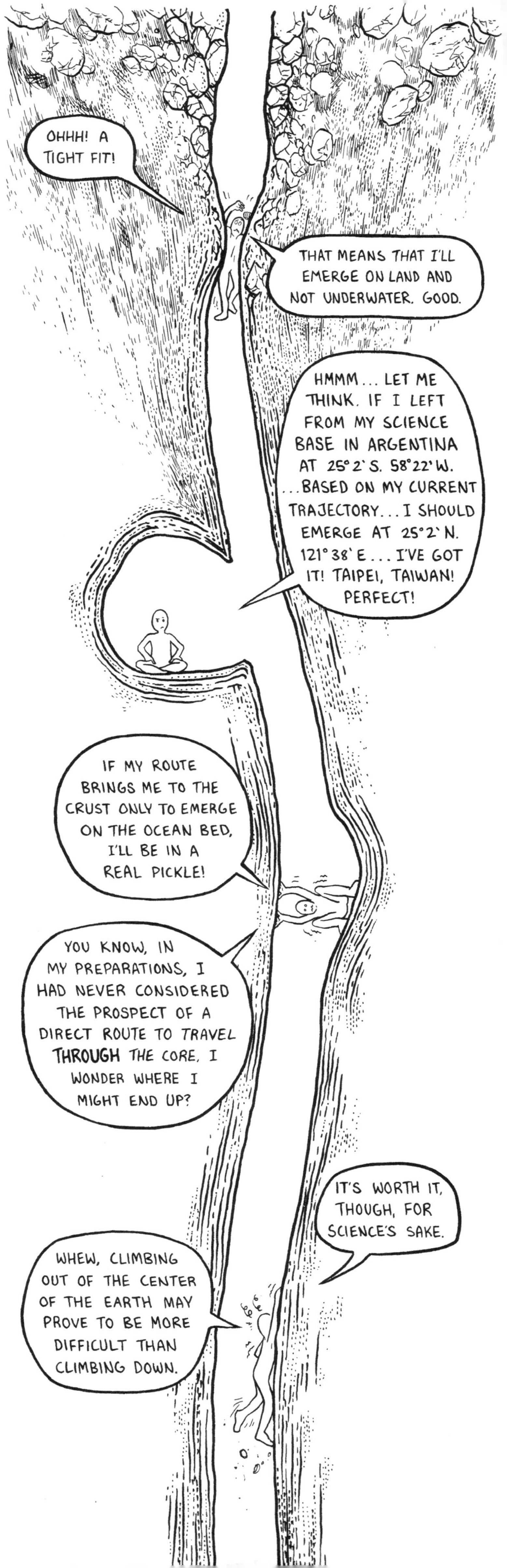
WHEW, CLIMBING OUT OF THE CENTER OF THE EARTH MAY PROVE TO BE MORE DIFFICULT THAN CLIMBING DOWN.
IT'S WORTH IT, THOUGH, FOR SCIENCE'S SAKE.
YOU KNOW, IN MY PREPARATIONS, I HAD NEVER CONSIDERED THE PROSPECT OF A DIRECT ROUTE TO TRAVEL **THROUGH** THE CORE. I WONDER WHERE I MIGHT END UP?
IF MY ROUTE BRINGS ME TO THE CRUST ONLY TO EMERGE ON THE OCEAN BED, I'LL BE IN A REAL PICKLE!
HMMM... LET ME THINK. IF I LEFT FROM MY SCIENCE BASE IN ARGENTINA AT 25°2' S. 58°22' W. ...BASED ON MY CURRENT TRAJECTORY... I SHOULD EMERGE AT 25°2' N. 121°38' E... I'VE GOT IT! TAIPEI, TAIWAN! PERFECT!
THAT MEANS THAT I'LL EMERGE ON LAND AND NOT UNDERWATER. GOOD.
OHHH! A TIGHT FIT!

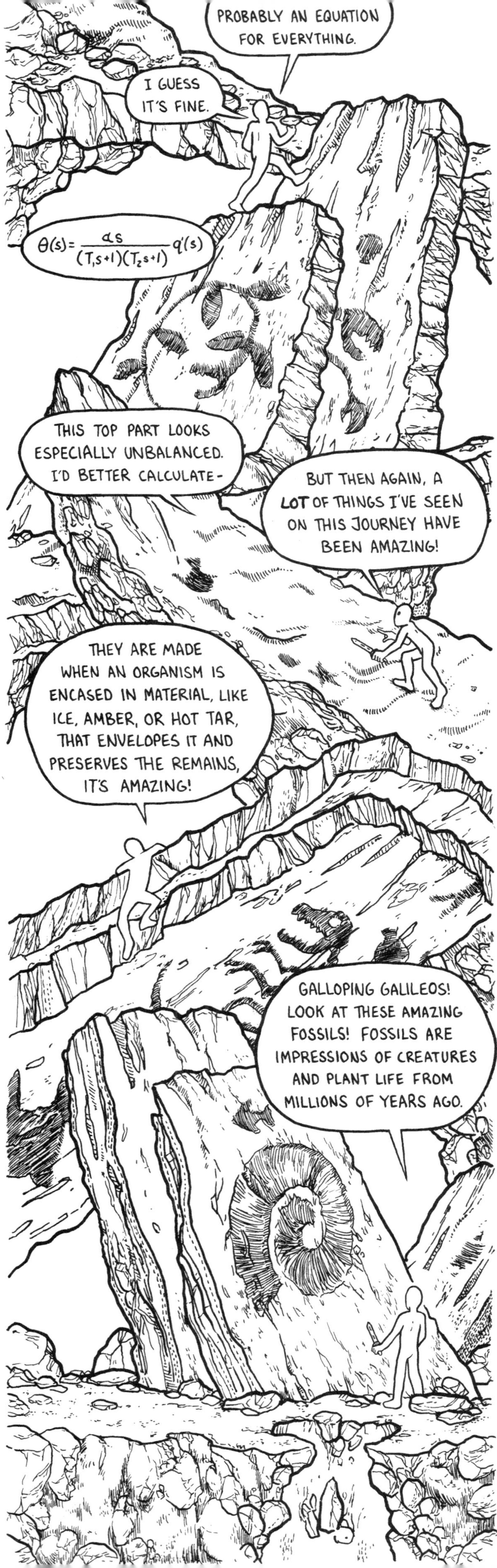
GALLOPING GALILEOS! LOOK AT THESE AMAZING FOSSILS! FOSSILS ARE IMPRESSIONS OF CREATURES AND PLANT LIFE FROM MILLIONS OF YEARS AGO.
THEY ARE MADE WHEN AN ORGANISM IS ENCASED IN MATERIAL, LIKE ICE, AMBER, OR HOT TAR, THAT ENVELOPES IT AND PRESERVES THE REMAINS. IT'S AMAZING!
BUT THEN AGAIN, A **LOT** OF THINGS I'VE SEEN ON THIS JOURNEY HAVE BEEN AMAZING!
THIS TOP PART LOOKS ESPECIALLY UNBALANCED. I'D BETTER CALCULATE-
$\theta(s) = \frac{\alpha s}{(T_1 s+1)(T_2 s+1)} q'(s)$
I GUESS IT'S FINE.
PROBABLY AN EQUATION FOR EVERYTHING.

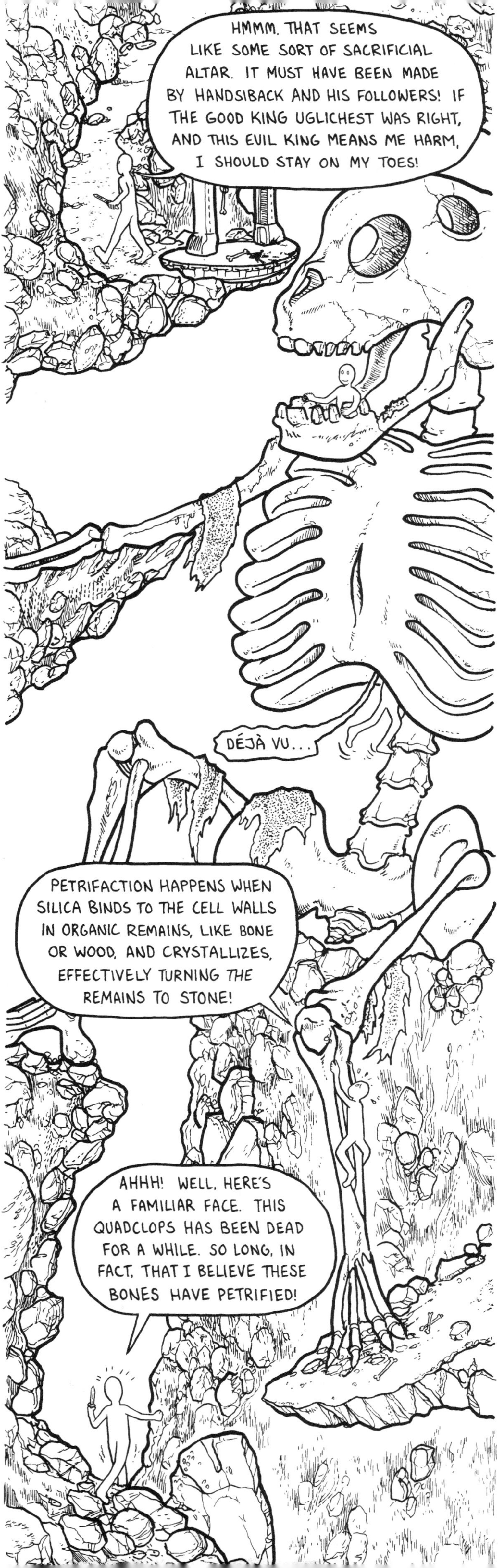
HMMM. THAT SEEMS LIKE SOME SORT OF SACRIFICIAL ALTAR. IT MUST HAVE BEEN MADE BY HANDSIBACK AND HIS FOLLOWERS! IF THE GOOD KING UGLICHEST WAS RIGHT, AND THIS EVIL KING MEANS ME HARM, I SHOULD STAY ON MY TOES!
DÉJÀ VU...
PETRIFACTION HAPPENS WHEN SILICA BINDS TO THE CELL WALLS IN ORGANIC REMAINS, LIKE BONE OR WOOD, AND CRYSTALLIZES, EFFECTIVELY TURNING THE REMAINS TO STONE!
AHHH! WELL, HERE'S A FAMILIAR FACE. THIS QUADCLOPS HAS BEEN DEAD FOR A WHILE. SO LONG, IN FACT, THAT I BELIEVE THESE BONES HAVE PETRIFIED!

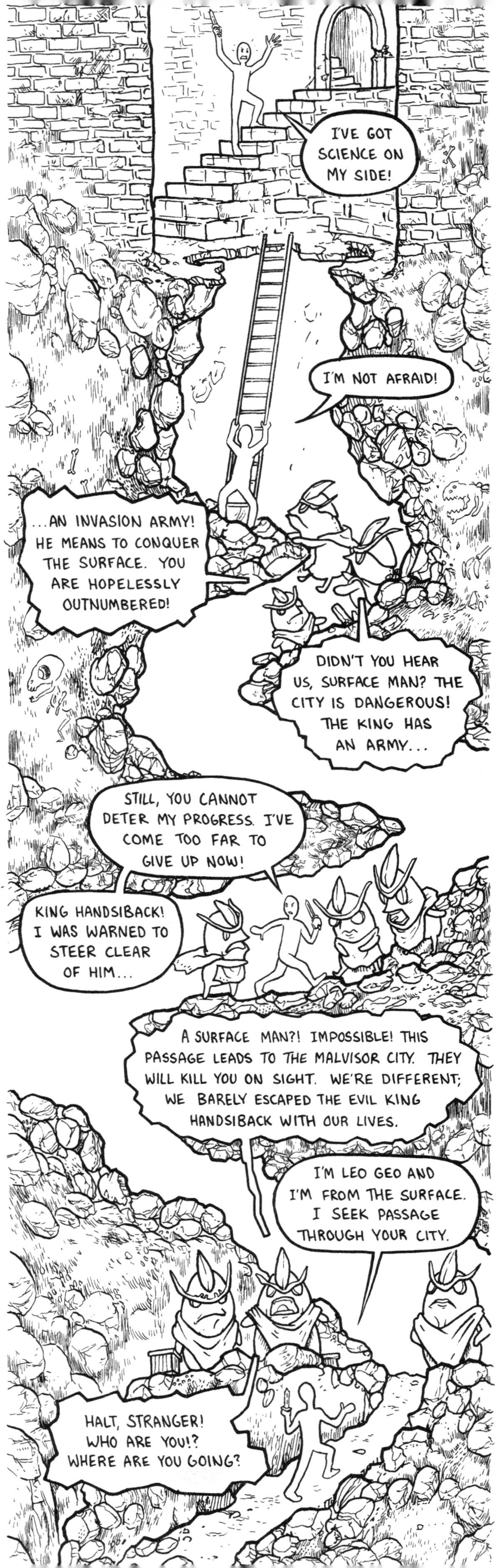
HALT, STRANGER! WHO ARE YOU!? WHERE ARE YOU GOING?
I'M LEO GEO AND I'M FROM THE SURFACE. I SEEK PASSAGE THROUGH YOUR CITY.
A SURFACE MAN?! IMPOSSIBLE! THIS PASSAGE LEADS TO THE MALVISOR CITY. THEY WILL KILL YOU ON SIGHT. WE'RE DIFFERENT; WE BARELY ESCAPED THE EVIL KING HANDSIBACK WITH OUR LIVES.
KING HANDSIBACK! I WAS WARNED TO STEER CLEAR OF HIM...
STILL, YOU CANNOT DETER MY PROGRESS. I'VE COME TOO FAR TO GIVE UP NOW!
DIDN'T YOU HEAR US, SURFACE MAN? THE CITY IS DANGEROUS! THE KING HAS AN ARMY...
...AN INVASION ARMY! HE MEANS TO CONQUER THE SURFACE. YOU ARE HOPELESSLY OUTNUMBERED!
I'M NOT AFRAID!
I'VE GOT SCIENCE ON MY SIDE!

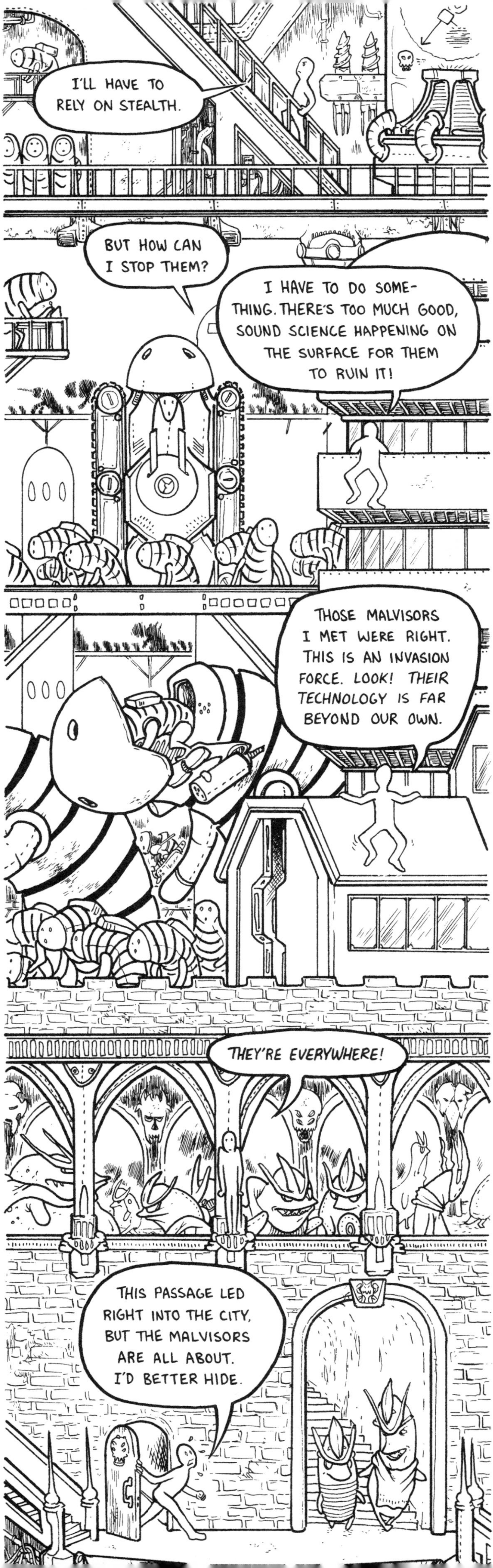
THIS PASSAGE LED RIGHT INTO THE CITY, BUT THE MALVISORS ARE ALL ABOUT. I'D BETTER HIDE.
THEY'RE EVERYWHERE!
THOSE MALVISORS I MET WERE RIGHT. THIS IS AN INVASION FORCE. LOOK! THEIR TECHNOLOGY IS FAR BEYOND OUR OWN.
I HAVE TO DO SOME-THING. THERE'S TOO MUCH GOOD, SOUND SCIENCE HAPPENING ON THE SURFACE FOR THEM TO RUIN IT!
BUT HOW CAN I STOP THEM?
I'LL HAVE TO RELY ON STEALTH.

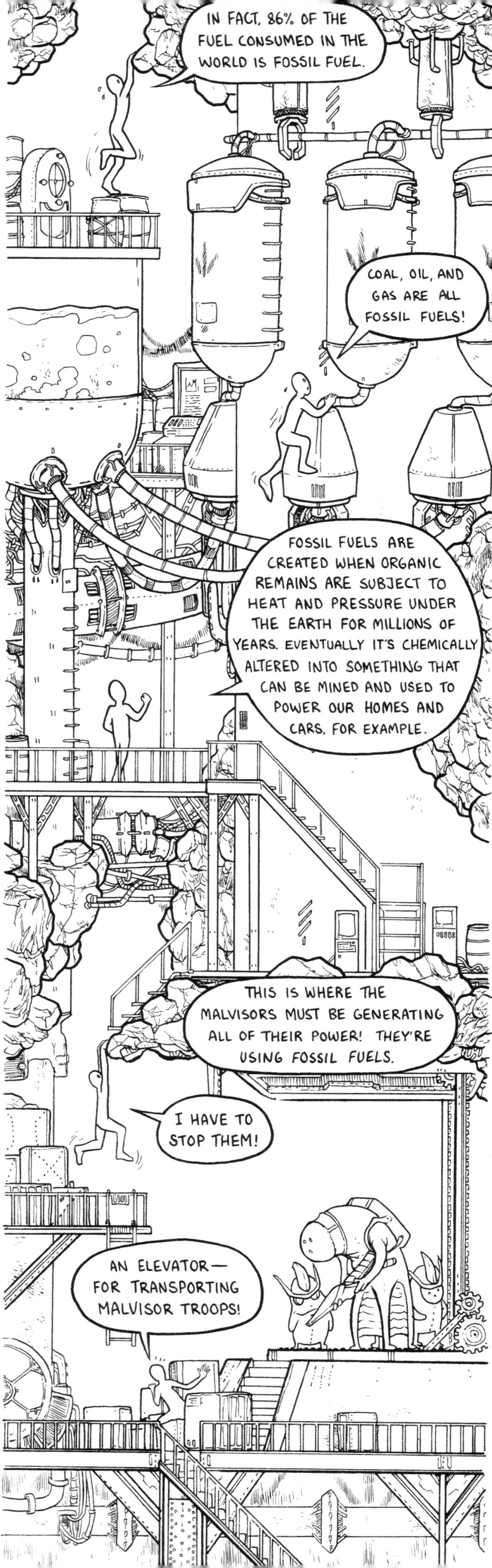
IN FACT, 86% OF THE FUEL CONSUMED IN THE WORLD IS FOSSIL FUEL.
COAL, OIL, AND GAS ARE ALL FOSSIL FUELS!
FOSSIL FUELS ARE CREATED WHEN ORGANIC REMAINS ARE SUBJECT TO HEAT AND PRESSURE UNDER THE EARTH FOR MILLIONS OF YEARS. EVENTUALLY IT'S CHEMICALLY ALTERED INTO SOMETHING THAT CAN BE MINED AND USED TO POWER OUR HOMES AND CARS, FOR EXAMPLE.
THIS IS WHERE THE MALVISORS MUST BE GENERATING ALL OF THEIR POWER! THEY'RE USING FOSSIL FUELS.
I HAVE TO STOP THEM!
AN ELEVATOR— FOR TRANSPORTING MALVISOR TROOPS!

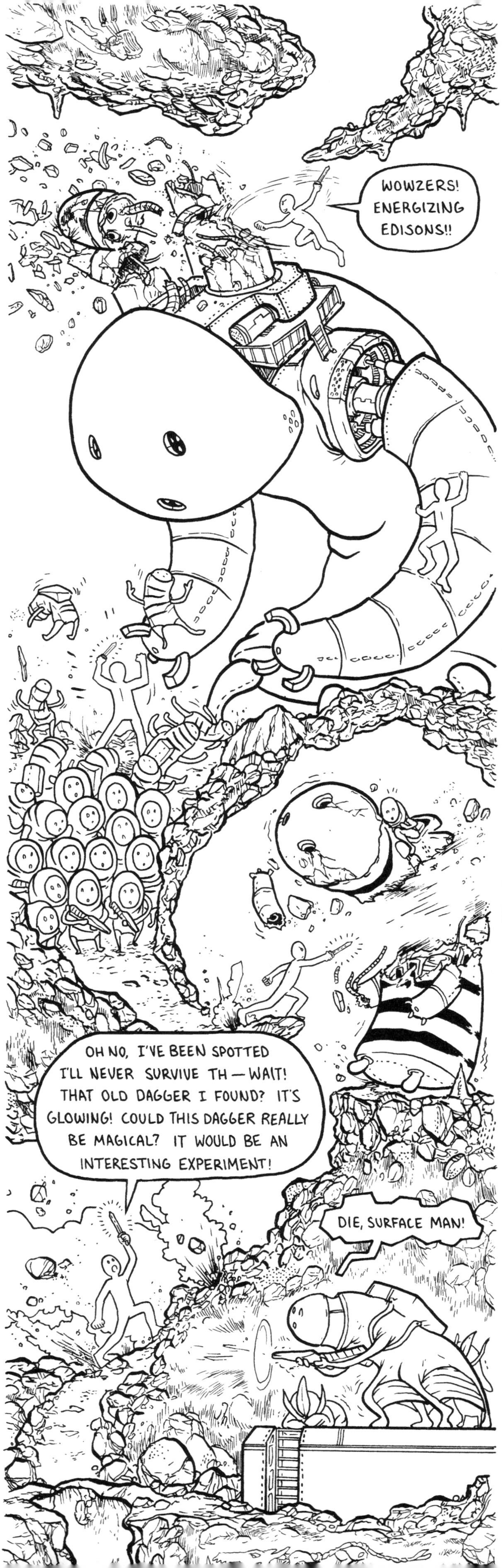
WOWZERS! ENERGIZING EDISONS!!
OH NO, I'VE BEEN SPOTTED I'LL NEVER SURVIVE TH — WAIT! THAT OLD DAGGER I FOUND? IT'S GLOWING! COULD THIS DAGGER REALLY BE MAGICAL? IT WOULD BE AN INTERESTING EXPERIMENT!
DIE, SURFACE MAN!

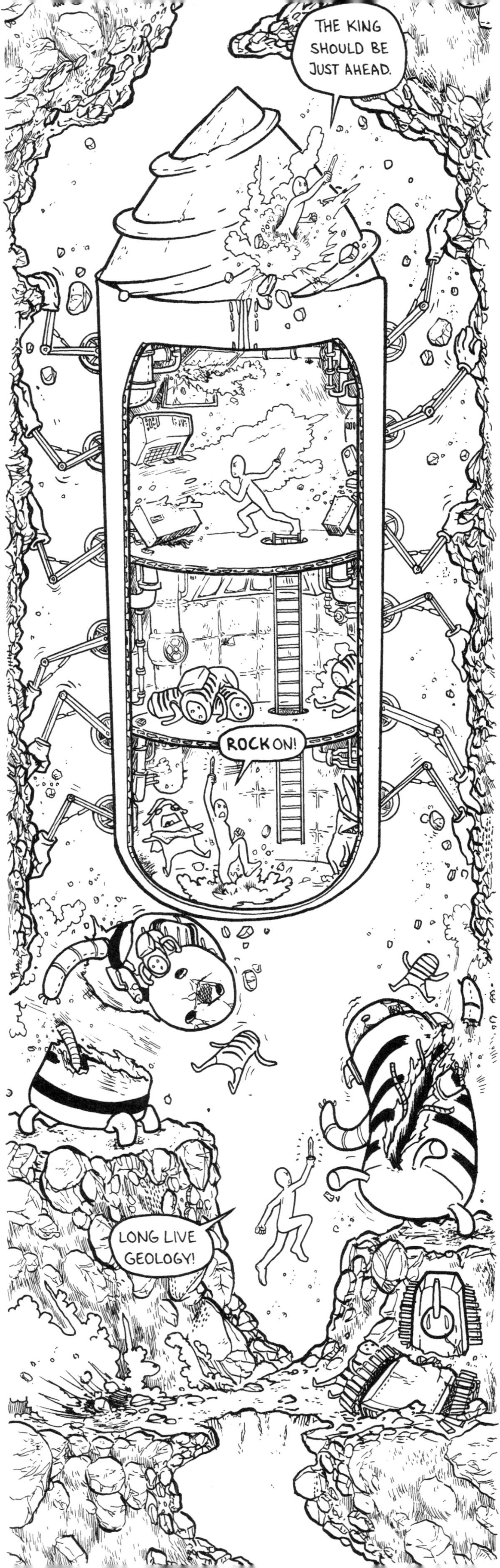
THE KING SHOULD BE JUST AHEAD.
ROCK ON!
LONG LIVE GEOLOGY!

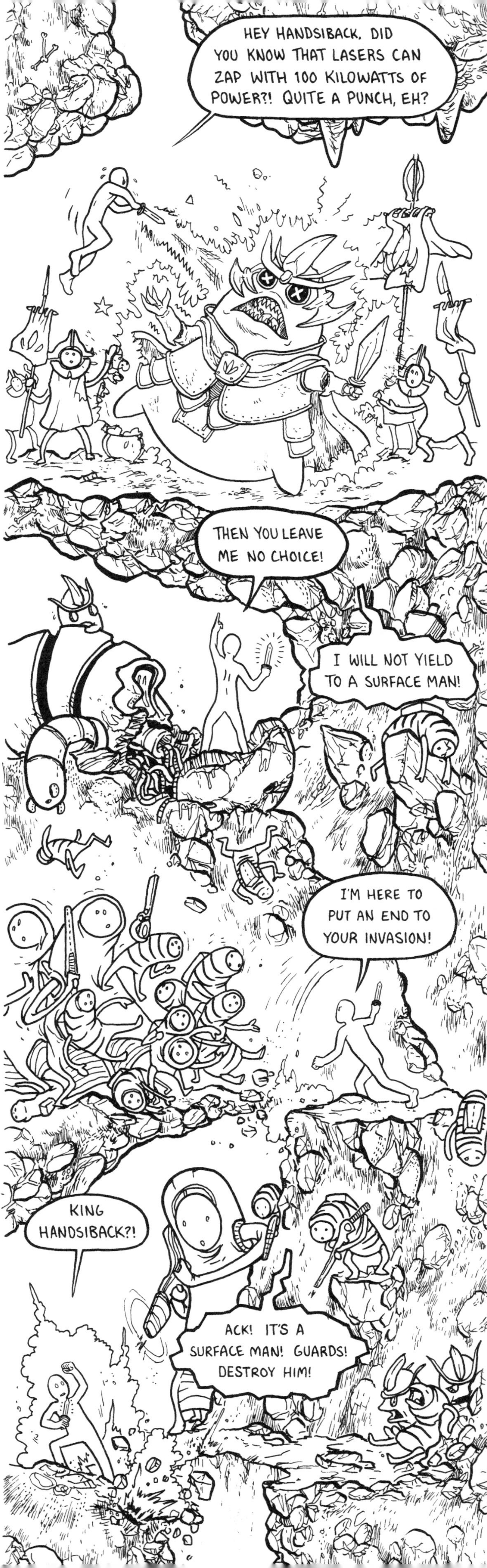
ACK! IT'S A SURFACE MAN! GUARDS! DESTROY HIM!
KING HANDSIBACK?!
I'M HERE TO PUT AN END TO YOUR INVASION!
I WILL NOT YIELD TO A SURFACE MAN!
THEN YOU LEAVE ME NO CHOICE!
HEY HANDSIBACK, DID YOU KNOW THAT LASERS CAN ZAP WITH 100 KILOWATTS OF POWER?! QUITE A PUNCH, EH?

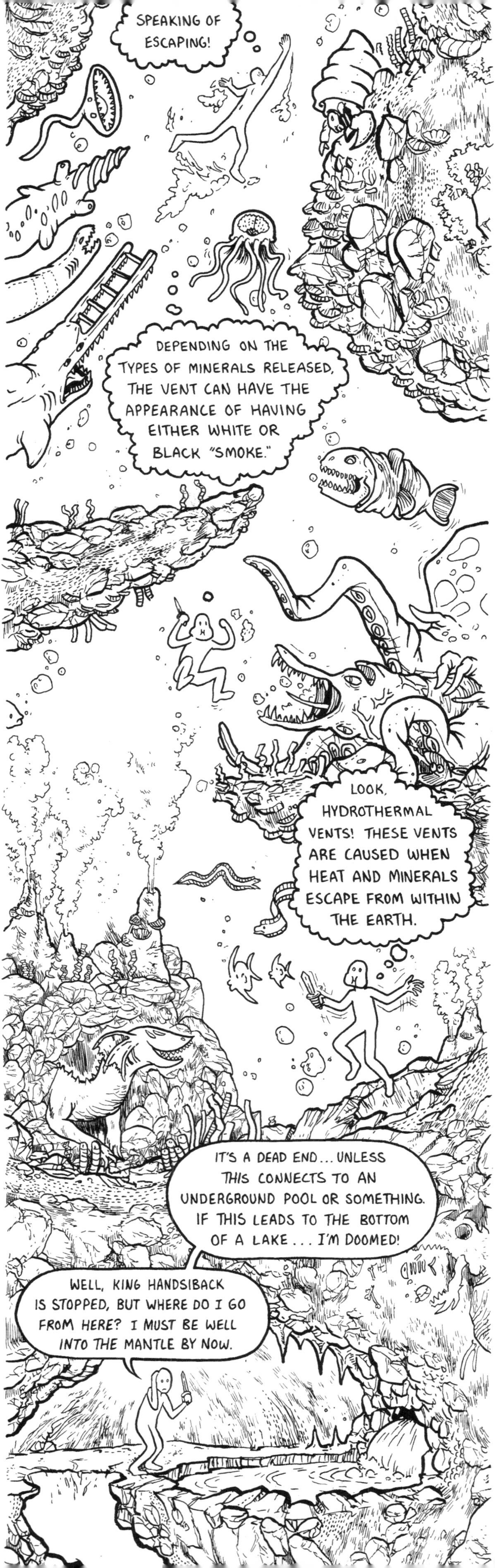
WELL, KING HANDSIBACK IS STOPPED, BUT WHERE DO I GO FROM HERE? I MUST BE WELL INTO THE MANTLE BY NOW.
IT'S A DEAD END... UNLESS THIS CONNECTS TO AN UNDERGROUND POOL OR SOMETHING. IF THIS LEADS TO THE BOTTOM OF A LAKE... I'M DOOMED!
LOOK, HYDROTHERMAL VENTS! THESE VENTS ARE CAUSED WHEN HEAT AND MINERALS ESCAPE FROM WITHIN THE EARTH.
DEPENDING ON THE TYPES OF MINERALS RELEASED, THE VENT CAN HAVE THE APPEARANCE OF HAVING EITHER WHITE OR BLACK "SMOKE."
SPEAKING OF ESCAPING!

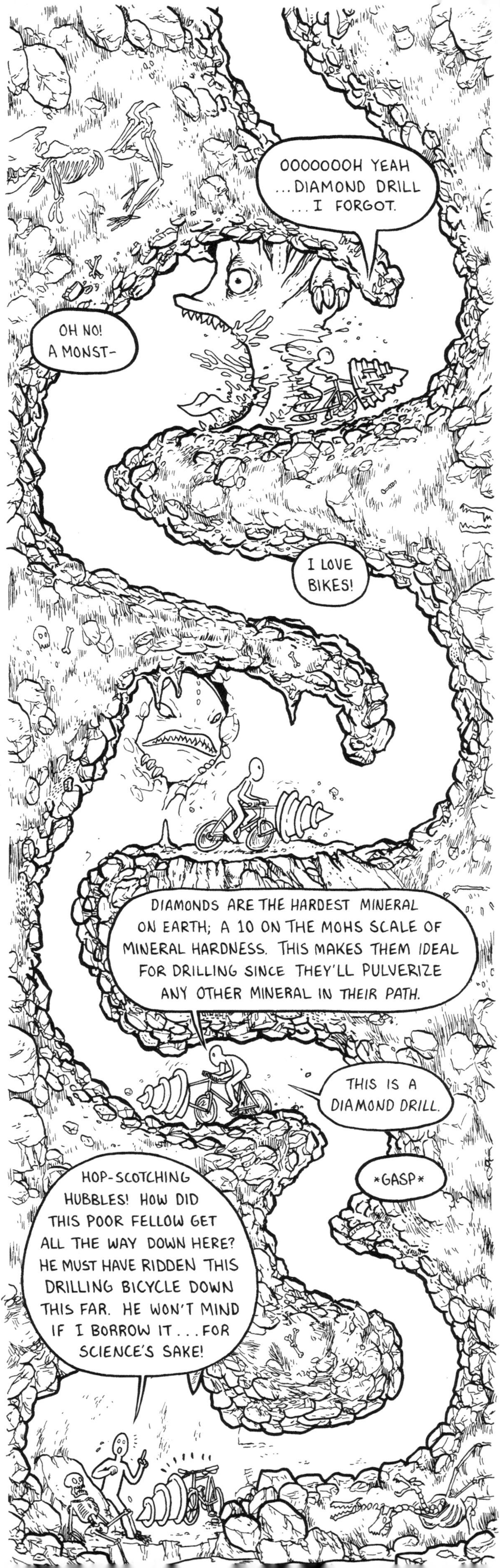
HOP-SCOTCHING HUBBLES! HOW DID THIS POOR FELLOW GET ALL THE WAY DOWN HERE? HE MUST HAVE RIDDEN THIS DRILLING BICYCLE DOWN THIS FAR. HE WON'T MIND IF I BORROW IT . . . FOR SCIENCE'S SAKE!
GASP
THIS IS A DIAMOND DRILL.
DIAMONDS ARE THE HARDEST MINERAL ON EARTH; A 10 ON THE MOHS SCALE OF MINERAL HARDNESS. THIS MAKES THEM IDEAL FOR DRILLING SINCE THEY'LL PULVERIZE ANY OTHER MINERAL IN THEIR PATH.
I LOVE BIKES!
OH NO! A MONST-
OOOOOOOH YEAH ...DIAMOND DRILL ... I FORGOT.

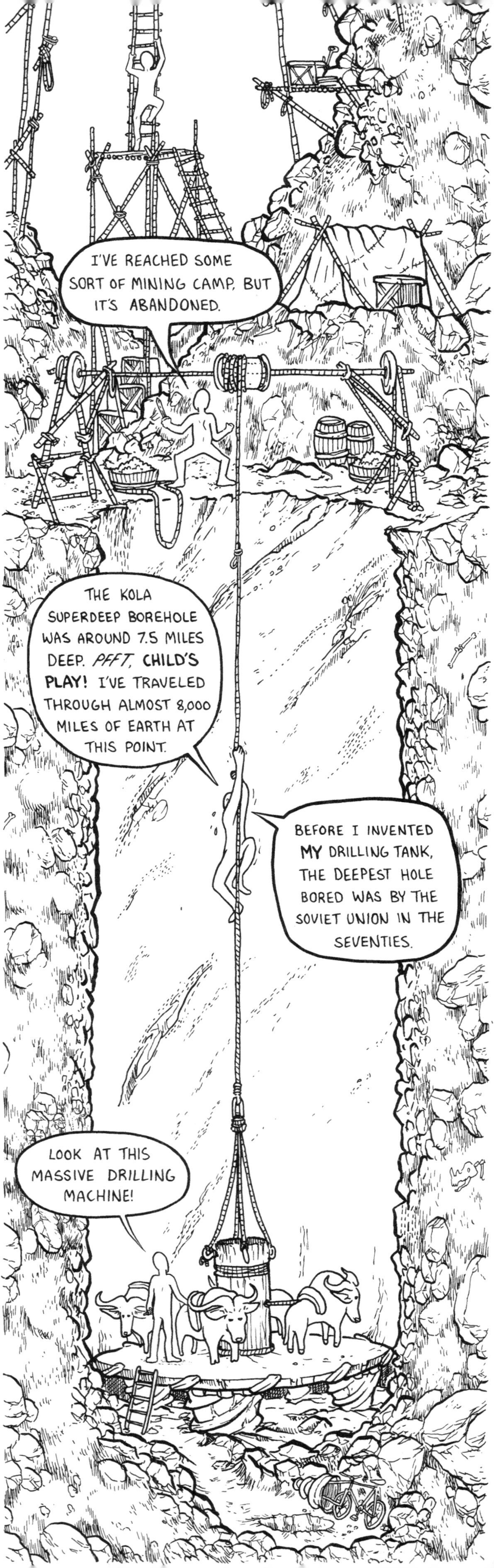
I'VE REACHED SOME SORT OF MINING CAMP, BUT IT'S ABANDONED.
THE KOLA SUPERDEEP BOREHOLE WAS AROUND 7.5 MILES DEEP. *PFFT,* **CHILD'S PLAY!** I'VE TRAVELED THROUGH ALMOST 8,000 MILES OF EARTH AT THIS POINT.
BEFORE I INVENTED **MY** DRILLING TANK, THE DEEPEST HOLE BORED WAS BY THE SOVIET UNION IN THE SEVENTIES.
LOOK AT THIS MASSIVE DRILLING MACHINE!

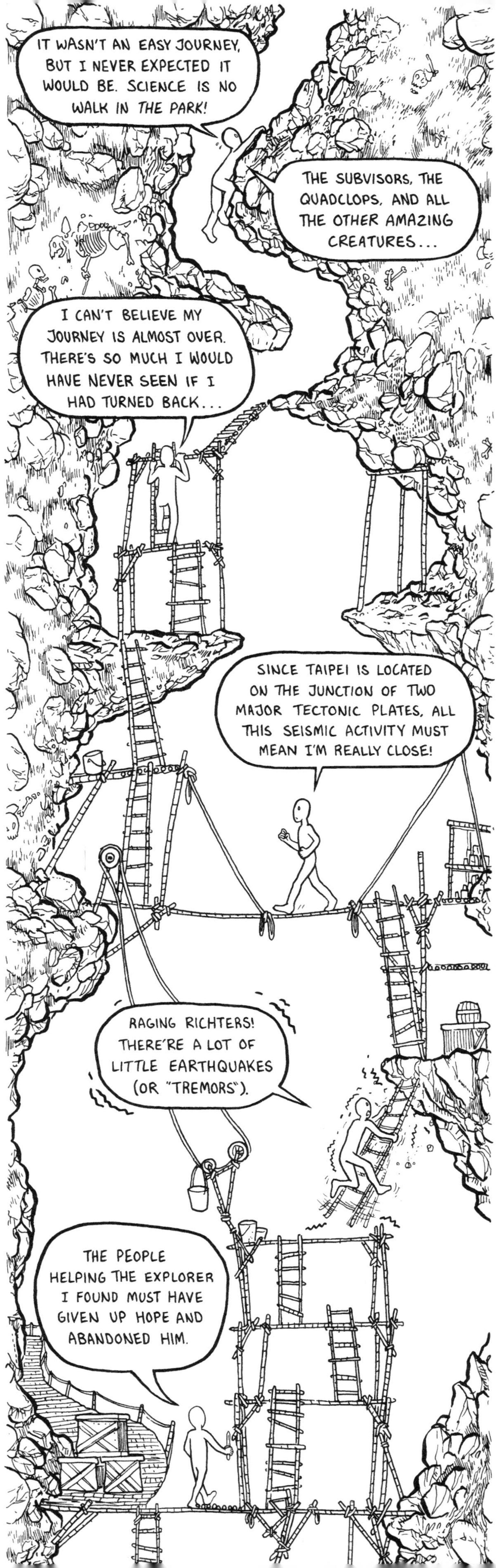
IT WASN'T AN EASY JOURNEY, BUT I NEVER EXPECTED IT WOULD BE. SCIENCE IS NO WALK IN *THE PARK!*
THE SUBVISORS, THE QUADCLOPS, AND ALL THE OTHER AMAZING CREATURES...
I CAN'T BELIEVE MY JOURNEY IS ALMOST OVER. THERE'S SO MUCH I WOULD HAVE NEVER SEEN IF I HAD TURNED BACK...
SINCE TAIPEI IS LOCATED ON THE JUNCTION OF TWO MAJOR TECTONIC PLATES, ALL THIS SEISMIC ACTIVITY MUST MEAN I'M REALLY CLOSE!
RAGING RICHTERS! THERE'RE A LOT OF LITTLE EARTHQUAKES (OR "TREMORS").
THE PEOPLE HELPING THE EXPLORER I FOUND MUST HAVE GIVEN UP HOPE AND ABANDONED HIM.

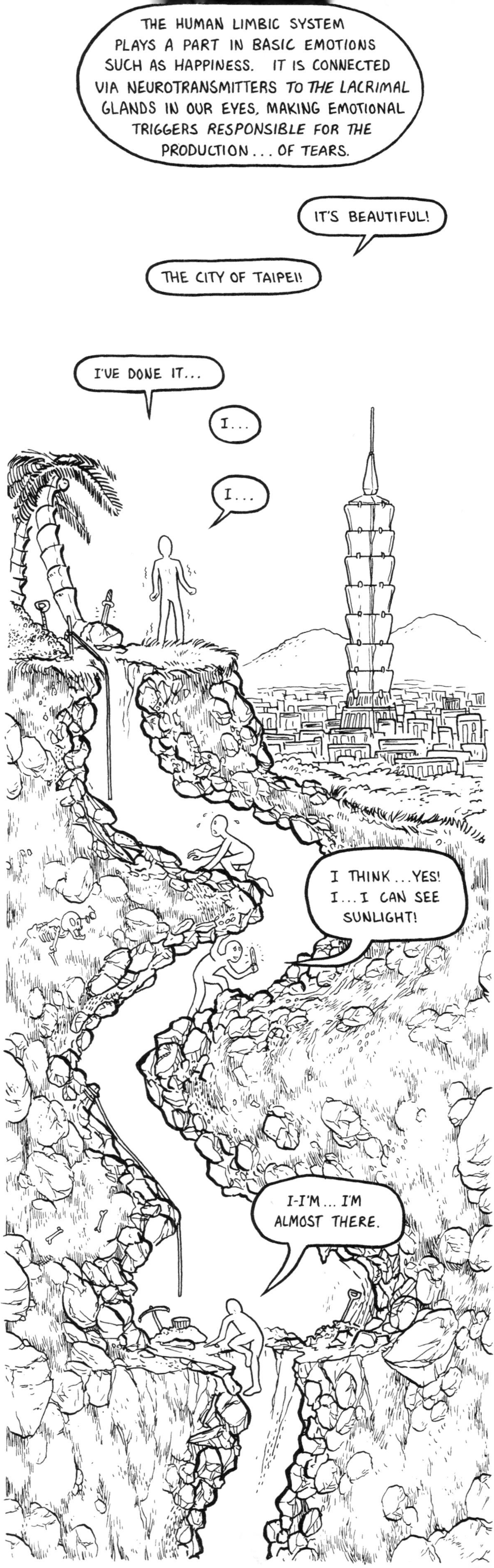
THE HUMAN LIMBIC SYSTEM PLAYS A PART IN BASIC EMOTIONS SUCH AS HAPPINESS. IT IS CONNECTED VIA NEUROTRANSMITTERS TO THE LACRIMAL GLANDS IN OUR EYES, MAKING EMOTIONAL TRIGGERS RESPONSIBLE FOR THE PRODUCTION . . . OF TEARS.
IT'S BEAUTIFUL!
THE CITY OF TAIPEI!
I'VE DONE IT...
I...
I...
I THINK...YES! I...I CAN SEE SUNLIGHT!
I-I'M... I'M ALMOST THERE.

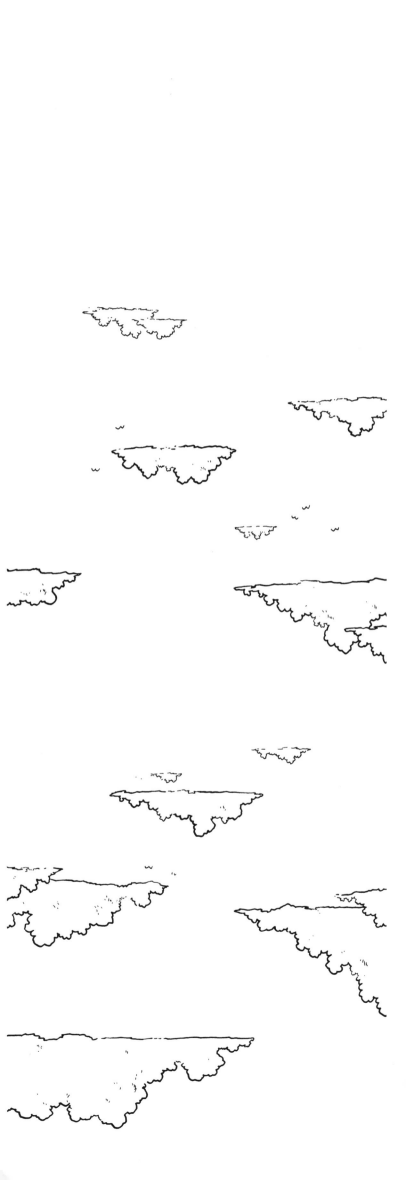

Katherine R, Joe L, Robyn C, CCS, my friends, family,
Maddrox, and Scamander. Also, thanks to
Ted Freshney, PhD for his expert review.

Published by Roaring Brook Press

Roaring Brook Press is a division of
Holtzbrick Publishing Holdings Limited Partnership
175 Fifth Avenue, New York, New York 10010

★ www.mackids.com ★

Cataloging-in-Publication
data is on file at the
Library of Congress.
ISBN 978-1-59643-661-9

Roaring Brook Press Books are available
for special promotions and premiums.
For details contact: Director of Special
Markets, Holtzbrick Publishers

First Edition 2012

Book design by Jon Chad
Printed in China
by Toppan Leefung Printing Ltd.,
Dongguan City, Guangdong Province

3 5 7 9 8 6 4 2